❀ Bride
at Eighteen

By the Same Author
The Best Wedding Dress
Christmas Cruise
Classmates by Request
A Crown for Gina
The Girl for Puerto Rico
Julie Builds Her Castle
Mrs. Darling's Daughter
Phoebe's First Campaign

Bride
at Eighteen

Hila Colman

William Morrow and Company   New York 1966

For my son Jimmy

Bride at Eighteen

1

AFTER THE MANY SUC-
cessive days of bright, icy cold January sunshine, the thaw
and the warm rain came as a relief. The campus reacted
to the change in weather as if one button had released
them all; girls huddled together under communal pon-
chos, giggling, sloshing their sneakers through the puddles;
the boys, their wet hair glistening, disdainfully ignored
the weather, visibly smug in their superiority to such trivia.

The professors were only too familiar with the pattern:
sodden students straggling into classes late; the unmistak-
able odor of damp wool, emanating from hundreds of
sweaters, permeating the halls; the students themselves
more talkative, restless, like children bored at the beach
and suddenly excited by the novelty and drama of a
storm.

Kate Minton watched the rain from her dorm window. It made her both nostalgic and homesick. In the little village of Hebron, Vermont, where she had been born and grew up, everyone had gathered in the Congregational Church during the previous summer and fall, offering up futile prayers for rain to break the drought. It had been pitiful to watch the streams dry up, the lawns turn brown, and the modest vegetable and flower gardens wither. Hebron was like an isolated pioneer community concentrating on its will to exist—everyone had been involved with the weather. All the villagers had been too preoccupied and intent to give any words or thought to the problems of the outside world of war and peace, civil rights demonstrations, marches, murders, or any event that did not touch upon their own immediate problem.

The door behind her banged open and closed, interrupting her thoughts. "Ugh, what a mess!" Her roommate Candy was kicking off her wet sneakers. "Of course, I got my beautifully typed paper wet. Barnes gave me a dirty look when I handed it in, but what could I do? I wouldn't type it over again for a million, besides it would be late. It's a good paper, and if he gives me any less than a B plus I'm going to holler. Are you coming to the teach-in later?" Candy was shaking the water out of her long blond hair.

"I hadn't planned to. I don't know anything about politics or foreign policy." Kate was dubiously eyeing the growing puddle around Candy's feet.

"That's the whole point of going. To learn something. College is where you come to get a broad education . . . isn't that what the books say? You've got to get out of this Vermont syndrome, Kate. There's a big world out there."

"So I've heard," Kate said drily. "But it's in too big a muddle for my poor brain. You get it straightened out and tell me all about it."

"Nuts to you," Candy said impudently, her snub-nosed, pert face wrinkled up disdainfully as she stepped out of her wet clothes. "That beautiful, idyllic village of yours is going to get blown right off the map one of these days without anyone even knowing what's happened to it. You're too pretty and smart to go on dancing in the dark."

"Why, the girl is positively lyrical! 'Dancing in the dark, till the tune ends. . . .' " Kate whirled around singing the melody. "My favorite song. Good grief, but you've made a mess!" Kate looked again at the puddle spreading around Candy's pile of wet clothes on the floor.

"Don't fret, I'll clean it up. But seriously, will you come tonight?"

Kate's dark blue eyes were teasing. "My great-grandmother was a suffragette and she went to jail for her trouble. Ever since then the women in our family have stayed out of politics. We're a simple, old-fashioned bunch. We stay home and knit, and make maple syrup. . . ."

"Yeah, yeah. I'm going down to the library. Meet me there at five." Candy had already put on a dry sweater and skirt and was halfway out the door. "We'll pick up some food at the Coop. See you later."

Alone in the room Kate gingerly skirted the water on the floor and went back to her perch at the window. It had been raining, too, the day she had arrived here at Branston University, a shy and scared freshman, her new flannel suit soaked and her hair dripping . . . that had been a year ago this past September.

Perhaps she *would* go to the teach-in. She had the sophomore blues, and it might be just the thing she needed to pull her out of them. "Dancing in the dark—" She hummed the tune softly to herself. Soon it would be spring and she wished she were in love.

The Student Union, often empty on a Friday night, was jammed with students. All sorts had turned out for the occasion: the so-called beatniks, bearded, with their dungaree-clad, pale-faced girls; the cashmere sweater girls hanging on to the arms of neat, crew-cut, closely shaven boys; serious students who fell into no category except that of being labelled intellectuals by their comrades; and frivolous girls and boys who thought of the teach-in as a new kind of lark and an excuse to stay up all night.

"I told you anyone who was anyone would be here," Candy said.

Kate was fascinated by the crowd. She hadn't expected such a crush. Many of the students were carrying placards in support of the United Nations, asking for peace, and Kate laughed at one sign that said, *Let's make love, not war.* "That's a sensible notion," she remarked.

"Hi." Candy was greeted by a cheerful, round-faced boy, Tommy Gargan, whom she had described to Kate as more friend than boy friend. "I see you brought Miss Hebron along." Kate was still teased about a discovery Candy had made, and gleefully advertised, that Kate had won a beauty contest back home when she was a senior in high school. Tommy introduced the boy with him, Mike Gordon, who was tall and had a dark, moody, but interesting face. "He's from Brooklyn, but don't hold that against him," Tommy said. "He can't help it. He was just born there."

"What's wrong with Brooklyn?" Kate asked innocently.

"Nothing," Mike said quickly. "Don't pay any attention to him. He doesn't even know that the best Irish families live in Brooklyn." Both boys laughed at what was apparently a private joke referring to Tom's Irish background.

"Let's find some seats," Tommy suggested, and the four of them made a dash for some empty ones in the back of the auditorium. Kate found herself sitting at the end next to Mike. "This is terrific," he said. "There hasn't been a turnout like this for anything this year. It's going to be an exciting evening."

"I hope not too exciting," Kate murmured, bewildered by the din of the dozens of separate, passionate discussions going on around her. The audience quieted down, however, when a professor stepped to the microphone.

For almost four hours the students listened attentively to several professors speaking on foreign policy and presenting various solutions to the war situation.

After the speakers finished, discussion was thrown open to the floor and questions were asked for. Then the excitement began all over again. Kate found the volatile passion of some of the young people around her unnerving. She wasn't used to hearing people express their opinions so strongly. Beside her, Mike Gordon was so eager to be heard he could hardly contain himself. His hand shot up, and she could feel him shaking with excitement. When he was finally recognized by the chairman, Kate admired his ability to express himself so clearly in front of such a large crowd, yet his words frightened her. She had always taken so many comfortable beliefs for granted. Her trust in the wisdom of elected public officials had been unquestioning, like her acceptance of all reporting she read in newspapers and magazines and her faith that whatever her country did was right, that it could make no mistakes. Yet there was Mike citing instances of bungling and errors, pointing out biased reporting. He seemed to be afraid of no one, no matter how high up in government circles, in his stinging denunciation of policy and tactics. His words left Kate shaken. What was there left to believe in, if he ripped all this away?

When they adjourned for an intermission to have sand-wiches and cold drinks, Mike kept close to Kate's side. "Well, what did you think of it?" he asked.

The noise in the main hall of the Student Union was deafening as the private arguments and discussions again took over. In one corner two boys had to be pulled apart when their differences turned to physical blows.

"I don't know what to think. Why do people get so

excited? Everyone wants peace, but they fight so with each other." Mike had to lean close to hear Kate's gentle voice.

"People feel strongly, and why shouldn't they?" Mike's eyes roamed around the huge room. "You can't sit on the sidelines. Everyone has to take a position today."

"But why?" Kate too was eyeing the animated discussions and the frequently over excited gestures of the students. "After all, the people in government know more than I do. Who am I to tell them what to do?"

Mike shook his head impatiently. "The professors here know a lot too, and even in the administration there's not always agreement. The government officials have to know what the people think—they're not infallible. They can make mistakes, and do. I think people have to speak out and fight for what they believe in."

"What do you believe in?" Kate asked.

"I believe in the people. People make a country. People have to make the government do what they want." Mike's intensity was like that of a boxer triggered for a showdown.

"I guess I'm not a fighter," Kate said.

"But you can't live with your head in the sand."

"I suppose not. . . . Candy calls it dancing in the dark, that's what she accuses me of doing. But I like dancing in the dark. I guess I'm just a cave dweller, or a nest builder. I like to be left alone."

"But you're not going to be left alone," Mike said, his dark eyes meeting hers. "For one thing, you're too pretty. I suppose you want to get married and have a lot of babies. But you won't be able to do it if the world gets blown up."

Kate laughed. "I guess I just want to make the most of my world while it's still here. Sure I want to get married and have babies—and if the world gets blown up, well, then it will. I don't think I can stop it, so I may as well enjoy it while I can."

"That's a pretty shortsighted point of view. I suppose it's all right with you if other people fight for your world?" Mike looked at her inquiringly.

Kate saw that he was serious. "That is their privilege," she said soberly. Then her eyes twinkled. "Maybe I'm old-fashioned, and I think the men should do the fighting and the women should stay home."

"That's worse than old-fashioned! That's downright subversive." Mike laughed with her.

"The awful thing is, I'm more serious than you think," Kate said wryly. "A boy like you must think I'm a real kook," she added, a slightly wistful note in her voice.

"In a way," Mike said frankly. "But you're so soft and

feminine it kind of goes together and seems right. I like kooks," he said, and his eyes made her turn away in embarrassment.

Candy and Tom, who had drifted away in the crowd, now pushed their way back to join them. "Are you staying for the seminars?" Candy asked Kate.

Kate could feel Mike's intent eyes on her as he waited for her answer. "Yes, I think I will," she said. "I've gone this far, I may as well hear the rest of it."

"Good girl," Mike said, pulling her arm through his.

It was a cold dawn when the seminars broke up. The rain had stopped, but the campus was shrouded in an eerie mist that, partially concealing the old stone buildings, made them look like medieval castles. "It's so beautiful," Kate murmured, feeling stimulated and amazingly wide-awake after the all-night session.

"I'm starved," Mike said.

"Let's go dig up some breakfast," Tom suggested. They piled into his car and drove to a nearby coffee shop that stayed open all night. The four of them wolfed down dozens of pancakes and drank hot coffee. Kate kept silent while the other three continued the discussions of the night, but when they were finished eating all four of them became unbearably sleepy.

The boys dropped Candy and Kate off at their dorm. "What did you think of Mike?" Candy asked, as the girls got ready for bed.

Kate didn't answer for a minute or two. Then she spoke in a low, deliberate voice. "I think he is the most irritating, fascinating, interesting, and annoying boy I have ever met. I know he thinks I'm simpleminded, but I think I could fall in love with him—although he certainly gets me mad."

Candy sat up in bed. "You are incredible. I just don't believe you, I really don't. I wouldn't have dreamed you'd fall for Mike Gordon. You're so full of contradictions! But I'm afraid you're right—I don't think you're his type."

"Maybe not," Kate said. She added sleepily, "But maybe that's in my favor."

2

IT WAS THREE DAYS later that Candy said to Kate, "I know why you find Mike so irritating. It's because he makes you think."

"Thanks a lot. You really do take me for a simpleton, don't you?" She was concentrating on gluing together two small rocks that were going to be made into a doll paperweight for her mother. "I'm going to use some of that yellow wool for her hair . . . she'll be real zany."

"You're not a simpleton," Candy said, "but Mike is brilliant. He's on the dean's list—he'll probably graduate magna cum laude. You don't have to be on the defensive about learning a thing or two from him."

Kate looked up from the table where she was working. "Honey child, I'm not on the defensive, you are. You keep asking me to join things. I'm not a joiner, and I'm not political. I'm just a simple girl from Vermont."

"That's what you think! Like I'm a simple girl from San Francisco. There are no simple girls anymore. The point is, lovey, you talk about majoring in sociology or psychology—and you did write that stunning paper on the migratory workers, so you *do* have a brain—but you simply can't be anything if you don't care what's going on in the world."

"I never said I didn't care. I merely said I didn't think I could do anything about it. There is a difference."

"I don't see it. If you care, you've *got* to do something."

"Like what? Like listen to Mike?"

"That's just the beginning."

Kate laughed. "Maybe that's what I'm afraid of," she said. "Come here, Candy, and hold this together while I make the hair."

Candy's face was grumpy as she permitted Kate to change the subject.

It didn't take many days for Kate to realize that Mike was seeking her out in a determined and consistent manner. He had lunch with her, and he had dinner with her. He sat next to her in the library while they both studied, and when they were finished he took her to the Coop for a sandwich. She was flattered by the attention of a senior, but she was also a little afraid of this dark-eyed, moody boy. "You're so intense about everything," she said to him one night over a corned-beef sandwich. "I don't see how anyone can feel so passionately about so many things."

Mike laughed and shrugged his shoulders. "That's the way I am. I live hard."

That same night Mike told her that he was planning to go home to Brooklyn for a weekend soon and he invited her to come with him. He explained easily that he wanted to show her New York, since she had only been to the city twice in her life and for very brief visits. He was persuasive and gay about the various places he would take her to—a certain coffee shop on Macdougal Street, a Chinese restaurant on Pell Street, the Degas horses in the Metropolitan Museum of Art, the Guggenheim Museum, the pushcarts on Orchard Street, and the Seagram building on Park Avenue—the list sounded like a full week of sightseeing to Kate. He was friendly and noncommittal in his argument, yet Kate sensed a motivation underneath his lightness that put her off. It occurred to her that he might want to see what she was like away from the campus and in his own setting, and that he wanted her to meet his family.

Mike talked about his family in the same way that he talked about everything else, volubly and intensely. His father, he said, was a disappointed musician turned insurance salesman out of necessity to make a living. "The last man in the world to be out selling," Mike explained. "He worries more about the customer either spending too much or getting gypped than he does about making a buck. He's a dreamer, an idealist. My mother comes from a bunch of intellectuals. She tries to be practical, but she isn't much better at it than my father. At the moment, my kid sister—she goes to the public high in Brooklyn— seems to have only clothes and boys on her little mind. But I think you'd like my father—he's much more gentle than I am. And my mother's an awfully good cook."

Kate gave considerable thought to Mike's invitation over a period of days, but in the end she declined it.

"Kate," Candy expostulated, "what are you afraid of? You'll be very well chaperoned by his parents, I can tell you that."

"I'm not worried about being chaperoned," Kate said irritably, "I can take care of myself—it's just, well, I guess I'm afraid of the whole situation. Mike is a terrific boy and I could fall madly in love with him in a minute, but it wouldn't work. Our backgrounds are so different. We don't think the same. . . . And besides, he'll be graduating in June and I'll probably never see him again, so where would I be? Here, and brokenhearted. No, I think I'll play it safe."

"Of course—if falling in love is purely an intellectual process for you!" Candy said with amused superiority. "I don't believe you at all. I think you're in love with Mike—you talk about him all the time—and I don't think it matters at all that he's political and you fight like anything not to be, or that his background is different from yours. You're both independent of your families anyway, and I don't know why you're resisting him so much. He's mad about you, anyone can see that."

"He hasn't said it," Kate said, and then smiled at her own giveaway.

Candy hooted. Then she added soberly, "Maybe he's shy too, and maybe he needs some encouragement before he opens his mouth."

"Maybe," Kate said.

The weekend that Mike went home was a tortuous one for Kate. She realized how used she had got to spending all her extra time with him, and how much fun they had together. She had discovered early in their friendship that he was not always serious: he had a great capacity for being silly and gay, and for enjoying himself enormously. To Kate his vitality was perhaps his greatest attraction— the way he happily squeezed every ounce out of life, whether it was a movie he was watching, a record he was playing, a walk in the woods, or the food he was eating. Everything mattered. If he was interested at all, he went the whole way; whatever he wasn't interested in, he dropped unhesitatingly, not wanting to waste his time.

Kate spent the weekend shaking off some of the boys she had dated before Mike came along and worrying about where she was headed. Though it was still March, there was a breath of spring on the New England campus, and she found the sweet freshness of it unbearably lovely. She kept seeing herself and Mike walking hand in hand around the streets of New York, laughing, talking, sitting in a coffee house, going through a museum, strolling up Fifth Avenue. . . .

Was she a fool or was she being smart? Was she, as Candy accused her of being, afraid of life, afraid of taking a chance? Did she only want to stick to the safe and the familiar—no matter how dull?

Mike came back earlier than she had expected on Sunday, and Kate made no attempt to hide her joy. "It was lonesome without you," she said to him.

"Why do you think I came back so early? I wanted to see you. My mother said I didn't talk about anything else all weekend, just Kate, Kate, and more Kate. Hey, I think I'm in love." Mike was still holding her in his arms, his lips smiling but his eyes serious. "Kate, I'm in love."

Kate's face was crinkled into a smile. "Me too. It's awful, isn't it?"

"What's so awful about it?"

"We're so different," she said.

Mike laughed. "I'd hate to fall in love with someone like me. I'm glad you're different." He kissed her with an urgency and tenderness that made her almost want to cry. The still unfamiliar intensity of her own emotion left her shaken. She had never felt this way about anyone before, loving so much and having a sense of destiny about their meeting, as if it had all been ordained a long time ago that on a certain evening this girl from Vermont should meet this boy from Brooklyn.

"I have the oddest feeling," she said laughingly, but half-serious, "that fate had it all mapped out for me to go to that teach-in and meet you. I never felt fatalistic before. Maybe we knew each other in another life." She held him off at arm's length and studied his face. "You're not at all the kind of person I ever dreamed I'd fall in love with.

I always thought he would be a country boy . . . someone without much ambition who liked to putter around, a nice big shaggy-dog type of guy. I guess I never really thought about being in *love* with someone, of feeling so intensely. But then one couldn't be casual about you. People are always either going to hate you or love you."

"As long as you love me I don't care about people," Mike said. "But that country boy . . . is there one?"

"Oh, no. Not any real person. Just someone I made up in my head."

Kate cleared the decks with Candy so that she could cook dinner for Mike and herself that evening and serve it in their room. She told Mike to come back in an hour and a half. Working breathlessly, she raced through the dorm to gather together what she needed. Recklessly she "borrowed" a package of cream cheese that was in the hall refrigerator, dug up a can of minced clams, and made an appetizer. Mixing together an assortment of canned Chinese food and some fresh hamburger, she concocted a main dish, and she fixed a salad of sliced cucumbers and tomatoes, which luckily Candy had hid in their room. The only thing around to make for dessert was fudge, so fudge and coffee it was. The most work was getting the room cleaned up and setting the table. Hastily she cut up some colored paper and made several abstract artificial flowers for a centerpiece that she placed between two candles. Then she got herself dressed. She spent the last ten minutes putting on make-up and telling Candy to evaporate.

Mike was properly impressed by all her preparations. "You must be a magician," he said, "to produce this at the last minute on a Sunday night. You are going to make someone a very good wife." Their eyes met, but Kate laughed away his serious expression.

When they had cleaned up all the food between them and were drinking their coffee, Mike said, "I'll be graduating in a couple of months and going down to New York to law school. I don't want to lose you, Kate. What are you doing this summer?"

"I haven't even thought about it, really. I guess I'll go home to Hebron and lie on my hammock. I can read books."

"Why don't you come to New York?" Mike was leaning toward her, his eager face animated. "It would be a great experience for you. If you're seriously interested in sociology, I bet you could get a summer job in some community program and see what it's like. How about it?"

Kate's eyes widened. "I don't know. I guess I'd have to ask my mother. . . ."

Mike was clearly amused. "Kate, darling, you're eighteen, sometime over the summer you'll be nineteen—you'll be a junior in college—you don't have to ask anyone's permission to make a decision like that. It's up to you."

Kate's face became withdrawn. "You don't understand. I don't *have* to ask permission, but I'd want to talk it over with her. Things are different in my house. There's just my mother, you know, my father's dead—well, you wouldn't understand."

Mike took her face between his hands gently. "Don't shut me out, Kate. I'm not going to understand everything right away, but give me a chance. By the way," he added lightly, releasing her, "when are you going to invite me up to meet your mother? I'd like to."

"You don't want to come to Hebron," she said evasively.

"Why not? Of course I do."

"To see how the hicks live?"

"Don't talk like that," Mike said sharply. "I love you. I want to know all about you. I want to see where you live, where you grew up. I've got to know everything."

"There's not so much to know." She shrugged. "You can come up to Hebron any time you want."

"Do you love me, Kate?" His eyes held hers in a long look.

"Yes, I do," she murmured.

"Then don't give me a hard time. Don't push me away."

Kate sighed. "Loving isn't all that easy. I love you . . . but sometimes I wish we thought the same way. There wouldn't be so many obstacles."

"But that wouldn't be any fun! I think if two people speak the same language too much, it's dull. They don't have anything to bring to each other. I like having to learn all about you."

"And when you do, I suppose you'll get tired of me?" Kate smiled at him ruefully.

"Never, never."

3

KATE AND MIKE CHOSE the first weekend of spring vacation for Mike's visit to Hebron. Deliberately Kate was very casual when she wrote to her mother announcing that she was bringing a boy home for the weekend, emphasizing the fact that he was just "a friend who has never been to Vermont and wants to see what it's like." The only cautionary note she added was to ask her mother to please tell Judd, her younger brother, to behave himself. A waste of words, Kate thought to herself, but always worth a try.

Her own feelings about the weekend swung back and forth from a mood of high elation to a low point of nervous anxiety. What would Mike think of her mother, what would she think of him? How would he like their house, the village? She alternated between thinking that letting him come was probably the dumbest thing she had ever done and resigning herself to the fact that it doubtless had to happen sooner or later.

Fortunately, there wasn't much time to ponder about it. The days before spring vacation were hectic as she finished up overdue papers, tried to get her clothes into shape, and went on a buying spree in Boston for fabrics, since she intended spending most of her vacation time making a summer wardrobe for herself. She was barely ready before it was time to leave.

"I bet you and Mike get married," Candy predicted when the girls said good-bye to each other. Candy was off to visit an aunt in Philadelphia, since her home in San Francisco was too far away.

"Don't be crazy," Kate admonished her. "You get the wildest ideas."

"Well, I don't know. This business of going home to meet your family sounds pretty serious to me."

"Nonsense!" Kate wished Candy hadn't said that, since it was exactly what she was afraid her mother would think.

"Just remember that I want to be maid of honor," Candy said teasingly.

"You'll get married before I will. You'll have to be my

matron of honor when it happens." Kate hugged Candy affectionately. She was constantly aware of how lucky she was to have Candy for a roommate. The two girls were very different; Candy wanted to be in everything, while Kate preferred to watch from the sidelines and, if possible, not take sides. Yet they got along extraordinarily well, even when Kate teased Candy about her peripatetic passions and Candy became impatient with Kate's resistance to involvement. They were fond enough of each other usually to end up laughing at each other's weaknesses, and neither one of them pushed the other around.

Using lots of tissue paper, Kate carefully packed the funny little stone doll with the long yellow braids she had made for her mother, mentally keeping her fingers crossed that her mother would like it. Kate was never too sure what Mrs. Minton's reactions would be to anything; she was a woman with a multitude of minor prejudices, and as soon as Kate thought she knew them all her mother developed new ones. Kate had never forgotten one unhappy Christmas when she presented her mother with a sweater she had secretly been knitting for months—only to be told that while the sweater was lovely, it was a pity her mother couldn't bear the touch of wool. In tears Kate had dragged other wool sweaters and dresses out of her mother's closet, but Mrs. Minton waved them away airily, saying she was allergic to the kind of *fuzzy* wool that Kate had used. Mrs. Minton had told Kate to wear the sweater herself, but Kate had given it away to the first rummage sale that came along.

How could she possibly foresee the way her mother would react to Mike?

Kate was both amused and shy when she and Mike boarded the train together in Boston. She suspected by the way strangers, mostly old ladies, looked at them and smiled that they thought they were on their honeymoon. The idea was rather delightful to Kate. She basked in Mike's attentions as he bought her a magazine to look at, helped her off with her jacket, and carefully stacked her suitcase on the rack.

"You make me feel as if I'm going someplace exciting, instead of home to old Hebron," Kate said.

"But of course, that's because you're with me." Mike grinned at her.

"There always is excitement around you, isn't there?" Kate was no longer flustered by the frank admiration in Mike's eyes. She used to be embarrassed by his close scrutiny, but now she was able to accept the fact that he thought her beautiful and feminine, and she suspected that if he stopped looking at her that way she would miss it very much.

"You're the one who makes excitement," Mike said. "Everyone always stares at you. I'm glad you're my girl. I like to have a girl that people look at."

Kate pushed her fair hair back from her face. She didn't think she was pretty as much as attractive-looking. She knew her honey hair and blue eyes were striking with her almost olive skin, but she thought her cheekbones were too high, her neck too long, and her chest too boney. "Stupid details," Candy always told her, whenever Kate found fault with herself.

It was dusk when they pulled into the tiny, weather-beaten Hebron station. "It sure looks dingy," Kate said, eyeing the familiar scarred wooden benches and peeling paint. Now why did I say that? she wondered, feeling as if she had betrayed an old friend. She had made up her mind that she was not going to try to impress Mike this weekend. Let him see things, and her, as they really were, even at their worst if necessary. Let him see that she did come from a very simple country background, and even though she had won a beauty contest once and had made it to a top New England university (she was on the second dean's list), she was very different from his sophisticated New York friends. She was almost defiant as she pointed out meagre, one-block-long Main Street, with its barnlike Grange Hall looming over the few stores, surpassed in ugliness only by the faded, ancient post office.

"Here's Judd," Kate said brightly. Then she was horrified to see her younger brother scramble out of the shiny new family car wearing fancy boots and tight dungarees and sporting long, uncut hair. Mike's eyes were amused, but Kate suddenly saw Judd as almost a caricature of the country boy trying to look like the city slicker.

"Nice car you've got here," Mike said, shaking hands.

"Oh, this—it's nothing much. I go for a sports car myself. But nix for my old lady."

"Well, what's new around here?" Kate asked, as Judd, with a great deal of flourish, drove them off.

"Are you kidding? What can be new around this cemetery? It's dead."

Mike politely asked a few questions about Judd's school and so forth, but after a few of Judd's monosyllabic responses he gave up. Kate was positive, even before the car stopped in front of their small frame house, that the weekend was a ghastly mistake and she had been a fool to let Mike come up here.

Mrs. Minton greeted them at the door. She was a once pretty, faded woman whose graying hair was carefully set. She shook hands with Mike and kissed Kate. "What a pretty suit. Did you get it at Filene's? Patsy Thompson bought a beautiful suit when she was in Boston. She said she got it on sale, but I don't believe her. She always loves to brag about the bargains she gets, and I don't believe half of what she says. Take your friend upstairs, dear, and show him where his room is. We don't have any guest rooms," she said, turning to Mike, "you'll have to go in with Judd. I bought a beautiful roast for your dinner. I told the butcher I wanted only five pounds, but he always cuts it bigger. I don't know why, because what can you do with cold roast? It just gets wasted for snacks. You can't tell that butcher anything, though."

Seeing her mother now through Mike's eyes, Kate was mortified by her inconsequential steady chatter, but she also felt sorry for her. She knew her mother's interests were limited to the village gossip, her own household duties, and the third-grade class in the public school where she taught. Yet Kate had a protective feeling for her, for the hard time she had had bringing up Kate and Judd after her husband was disabled in a factory accident, and then later died of pneumonia. Mike was being polite, but Kate was sure that she could read his thoughts, and her conclusion that he was privately critical of Mrs. Minton offended her.

"This is the living room." She took Mike into a square, drab room that had a bowl of artificial flowers on a table and a couple of inexpensive Van Gogh reproductions on the walls. The outstanding feature of the room was a large, new-looking television set. There were no books; the only reading matter was a very neat pile of old *Reader's Digests* on the same table as the flowers.

"As you can see we are not a very literary family," Kate said in a forced, gay voice. "We put our money into durables like cars and television."

"Both very important items, I'm sure," Mike said gravely. He met her eyes for a minute, and then looked away.

Kate wished that they were alone so Mike could take her in his arms and tell her that what she was had nothing to do with this house or even with these two people. Her affection for them suddenly seemed quite removed from the reality of her being, as if it came out of a separate compartment that was unrelated to anything else.

"Doesn't the table look nice?" Mrs. Minton's eyes followed Kate around the room. "Mrs. Duncan, I have her

Sara in my class, gave me some new furniture polish to try. It goes on so easy and smooth. I was thinking that while you were home you could go over that old desk in your room. I bet it'll shine up real nice."

Not a word asked about school, about the trip home, not even a question in her eyes about Mike. He could have been anyone, a casual friend who had dropped in for a brief visit. Mrs. Minton was oblivious to everything except the tiny world in which she moved. Not that she didn't care—Kate was sure that in her own way her mother loved her children, and if anything bad happened to either one of them she would be heartsick—but whatever feelings she had were buried deep under layers and layers of pathetic absorption in insignificant trivia. Kate wondered if she would get her mother's attention if she blandly announced that she was in love with Mike. What a fool she had been, kidding herself that her mother would be concerned about her bringing Mike home or pretending to herself that she had to talk over her summer plans with her mother. Although, on second thought, if she told her mother that she intended to spend the summer in New York the announcement might come as a shock.

Kate opened her suitcase and, digging around a bit,

came up with the bundle of tissue paper that held the stone doll. She handed it to her mother.

Mrs. Minton looked pleased as she tore away the layers of paper, but when the little doll lay in her hands she seemed puzzled. "What is it?" she asked.

"It's a doll. A paperweight. I made it for you," Kate said.

"It's real cute," Mrs. Minton said. "But what do I need a paperweight for? I haven't any papers."

Kate turned away with a sigh. "It can be a decoration then," she said.

After she and Mike deposited their suitcases in their respective rooms, Kate suggested that they go out for a walk.

At least, she thought, as they went down the country road, the hills are pretty and the air is fresh and sweet. They both were silent for a while. "Well?" Kate finally said.

"Well, what?" Mike smiled at her. "What do you want me to say? I'm glad I came. Your mother is very sweet. I've been thinking there must be thousands of women like her, in thousands of little villages like this one all over the United States, who don't know and don't care what's going on. They're all tied up in their own little lives. They never see the *New York Times*. They care about what

they're going to have for dinner tonight and who's marrying who, and if there's a war going on someplace way off
they're sorry, but it doesn't touch them. Not until it's too
late. I wonder if the people in Hitler's Germany were like
them too. It's scary."

"But my mother teaches school. She *is* doing something," Kate said defensively.

"That makes it even worse," Mike said soberly. "What is
she teaching them? How to spell cat, c-a-t, how to add
two and two."

"What else do you expect her to teach in the third
grade?"

Mike shrugged his shoulders. "I don't know. Maybe
they should be taught right from the beginning not to say
automatically, 'I pledge allegiance to the flag. . . .' I wish
they could be taught to think, instead of repeating all the
old clichés."

"Think, think! People should be taught to love, that's
the important thing," Kate said spiritedly.

"Both. To think and to love." Mike pulled her arm
through his. "You can't spend the summer here. It would
be stifling. You've got to come to New York."

Kate's eyes clouded over. "I thought I'd talk to my
mother about it."

"Who are you kidding? I don't think your mother would

care." Mike's words were light, but his eyes were sympathetic.

Kate gave a deep sigh. "She would care only because it would be a jolt to what she expects, to her own routine. And also because some of her friends would be shocked at her daughter's spending a summer alone in New York."

"Those things don't matter, Kate," Mike said. "You're the one who counts, and you have to get out of here."

At supper that evening Mrs. Minton asked Kate if she would accompany her to a meeting of the Future Grandmothers.

"But I have a guest, Mom," Kate said in dismay.

"I'm sure the young man wouldn't mind staying here for a bit and watching television with Judd. There are some good programs on Saturday night," Mrs. Minton said.

Kate met Mike's eyes. "What are, or is, the Future Grandmothers?" he asked curiously.

"Why, it's just some of the women in the town, the younger ones, too—we like to bring our daughters. They do fine things for the orphanage and the hospital, some beautiful needlework." Mrs. Minton seemed mildly surprised that Mike didn't know about the group. "I suppose you live in the city." This sentence was the first one she had addressed directly to Mike during dinner.

"Yes, I do. Go ahead, Kate, if your mother would like you to go. I don't mind staying here with Judd."

Kate wished she could kick Mike, but he was sitting too far away at the round, Mission oak dining table. There was no way for her to get out of the meeting gracefully now.

An hour later, sitting next to her mother in a stiff circle of chairs, it suddenly occurred to Kate why Mike had been so agreeable to her going. He must have had an inkling of how deadly the evening would be and how she would react to it. There were a few girls her own age who had been in high school with her, girls who were already like their mothers, wrapped up in their marriage and their babies, interested in recipes and the mild village gossip. They asked her politely how she liked college, and that was the end of the conversation. Kate sensed that her mother liked to show her off because she was at college, but at the same time Mrs. Minton wanted her to follow the pattern of marrying a local boy and staying in Hebron.

You can't have it both ways, Kate thought to herself, watching the clock slowly ticking the minutes off. She had thought, too, that in spite of having a college education all she wanted was to come home and live the simple life.

But falling in love with Mike had changed everything. Perhaps, also, she had changed more than she realized, for sitting there that evening she knew that she could never be satisfied with what Hebron had to offer. She wanted a good deal more than the limited, dreary talk of these women.

They came home at ten o'clock, and while her mother and Judd went to bed, Kate stayed up with Mike to watch the eleven o'clock news. "Don't you stay down there late," Mrs. Minton said, as if Kate were a small child.

"Mike . . . Mike. . . ." Kate drew him to her when it was time to say good night. "You're right. I can't spend another summer here. I'll suffocate."

"I know." Mike held her close. "We'll work out something," he promised.

4

KATE SAT IN HER DORM room studying the catalogue, trying to choose her courses for the following year. Nothing sounded interesting, nothing seemed worthwhile. The thought of coming back in September without Mike was more than she could bear. This very morning he had gone down to New York to find an apartment for himself, while she had an appointment with her adviser. The situation didn't make sense.

Today was not the first time Kate had asked herself what she was doing at Branston U. She knew all the pat answers, of course. She knew that she needed a college degree to make any kind of career for herself. Her scholarship, which she admitted was a great privilege to have received, made her feel obligated to keep her marks up.

But she didn't know what she wanted to do or where she was headed. Though she talked about majoring in sociology, she didn't feel strongly about it. Was all this effort worth it? Would she be any better off when she finished—if she ever did?

Kate felt very depressed as she walked across the pretty campus to keep her appointment with her adviser. Sitting across the desk from him a few minutes later, trying to map out a program, it seemed to Kate that she was going through mechanical gestures that had little relationship to her.

"You'll have to decide on your major, Miss Minton." Mr. Caldwell looked at her through his rimless glasses. "What is it going to be?"

"I don't know. That's the trouble," Kate said dispiritedly. "I suppose I could major in English and let it go at that."

"You have more history credits," he said crisply. "Have you considered sociology?"

"Yes, I have, but I'm not sure I would know what to do with it."

"There are many kinds of work open in that field. I'm afraid you don't have the proper motivation." He looked at her accusingly.

"I know," Kate mumbled unhappily. She got up to go. "I guess I need to think about it some more. I hope I haven't wasted your time."

"You'll have to make up your mind in the next couple of days." He dismissed her with a nod.

As Kate had expected, the interview was far less than satisfactory. She had known before she had gone to see her adviser that she still had to take Biology 1 and make up her language requirement. Just thinking about either one of them bored her stiff. Outside the sun was blazing brightly in a glorious May day. It was a day to do something joyous and exciting, something terrific that would shake off her stupid depression about school and courses.

Suddenly she had a brainstorm. Mike had again asked her to come down to the city with him, but she had refused. Now, standing in front of the library steps, the sun warm on her head, she wondered why she had said no. The big clock over the library was striking a quarter past eleven. Mike had taken the ten o'clock bus. Why couldn't she follow him? She could call his home and leave a message that she was taking the one o'clock bus; she knew there was one, because he had mentioned it.

A weekend in New York with Mike! Kate ran across the campus to her dorm and flew up to her room. She grabbed a handful of change from the cup where she and Candy dropped odd nickels and dimes and went to the phone booth at the end of the hall. She didn't know Mike's home number, but she knew his father's name was Ben, and she knew his address. Kate's heart was beating nervously while she waited for Information to give her the number.

It suddenly occurred to her that Mike's mother would undoubtedly answer the phone—Mike wouldn't be there yet—and the thought made her feel shy and uneasy. What kind of a girl would Mrs. Gordon think she was, calling up and saying she was coming down for the weekend? She had almost decided to hang up when the operator's crisp voice told her the number was TR 9-5960. Kate scribbled the number on the torn pad hanging by the phone.

She hung up the receiver and stared at the number for a few minutes. It was tantalizing to have it there right in front of her, the door to an exciting, wonderful weekend with Mike. Not to use it would be silly of her, after she had gone this far. Hurriedly, before she could change her mind, Kate dialed the New York number.

The woman's voice that answered at the other end sounded tired. Falteringly but speaking quickly, Kate explained that she was Kate Minton, Mike's friend. Would Mrs. Gordon please give Mike a message when he arrived, that she was taking the one o'clock bus down to New York, and would he please meet her at the bus station at five?

There was a dreadful second of silence. Then, sounding somewhat apologetic for her hesitation, Mrs. Gordon assured Kate that Mike would get the message. "Providing, of course, he comes home before five," she added. There was another second of uneasy silence, then Mrs. Gordon said a bit stiffly, "I look forward to meeting you. Mike has spoken of you."

"Thank you," Kate said. The operator was asking for more money, and with relief Kate said, "I guess I'd better hang up."

It was too late now to worry about whether she was doing something terrible. She'd have to hurry to catch that one o'clock bus. Kate packed a suitcase quickly, went down to the Coop to cash a check, and grabbed a sandwich and a coke. Then she realized she had forgotten to leave a note for Candy and went flying back to their room. She got to the bus station, breathless, at five minutes to one.

On the bus she was all ready to relax and think about

what she was doing when the lady next to her started up a conversation. She was a sad, wispy woman on her way to visit her grandchildren. Apparently she hadn't had anyone to talk to for a long time and was determined to make the most of her captive audience. Kate smiled politely, nodded at intervals, and did her best to admire the sad-eyed children whose pictures the woman took out of her huge handbag to show off. By the time the bus arrived in New York Kate was in a nervous state of excruciating boredom and resentful that she hadn't had a chance to straighten out her own thoughts.

Mike was nowhere in sight. The station was a mad-house of people rushing to take five o'clock buses out of New York. Kate stood close to her suitcase, dizzy from watching the crowds, dismally thinking that if Mike didn't appear very soon she would take the next bus back to Boston. She felt the absolute fool for having done any-thing so wild as rushing down to New York this way. Maybe Mike hadn't got her message . . . maybe he didn't want her to come . . . maybe. . . . This time was the first in her life she had ever done such a thing, and she shouldn't have tried to be someone that she wasn't. Standing there alone in the dirty, noisy, crowded station, Kate felt irri-tated and frightened. She was annoyed with herself and with Candy and Mike. They were the ones who had been pressuring her to behave more boldly, to make commitments and to act upon them, not to be so reluctant to turn from the safe, familiar, and secure.

Now she had stepped out of character, she had done something bold, and this situation was the result. Tears of frustration were brimming up to her eyes when there was Mike, tall, bareheaded, rushing through the crowd to greet her.

"Oh, Mike!" The tears spilled over as he kissed her. "I thought you weren't coming."

"I didn't go right home, so I didn't get your message until late. I got here as fast as I could. Darling, it's wonderful that you came." There was no mistaking his delight.

Mike took Kate down into the subway at Times Square. She had never been in the subway during the rush hour, with men and women packed up against each other unashamedly, squeezing inside the closing doors as if making the train were their last chance for survival. "Is it always like this?" Kate clung to Mike's sleeve, fearful of being separated forever.

She was relieved to get out into the pale sunshine at the other end. They walked past a nondescript group of neighborhood stores and down a block of old-fashioned brownstone houses to the modern apartment house where the Gordons lived. Kate thought the self-service elevator quite smart-looking, and she nervously stopped to powder her nose and run a comb through her long hair before she let Mike use his key to open the door.

"You look beautiful," Mike said, kissing the tip of her nose before throwing open the door.

"Anybody home?" he called out gaily.

Mike's family appeared instantaneously, as if they'd all been sitting and waiting for this moment. Mike made the introductions. First his mother, a plump, round-faced woman with the same bright, dark eyes as Mike's, then his father, slim and pale, wearing a shirt with a monogram. Last Mike waved carelessly to Tina, his tall, boney sister, who looked Kate over with a frankly appraising eye.

Mr. and Mrs. Gordon welcomed Kate cordially, and Mike took her into his room, which she would use for the weekend while he slept on the living-room couch. "This room looks like you," Kate said, admiring the book-lined walls and the sturdy, simple modern furniture. She went immediately to examine the pictures on the wall, of Mike with the swimming team at camp and Mike in a football helmet at high school. "You haven't changed a bit," she told him laughingly.

The entire apartment seemed to be filled with books, in the living room, in the hall, in the dining area; the living-room table was piled high with magazines. The few pictures on the wall, Kate noticed with awe, were not prints at all but original oils and watercolors, and on the mantelpiece over the fake fireplace was a lovely sculptured head of Tina. Mike casually told her that his father, who had lately taken up sculpturing in his spare time, had done it. "When he isn't too busy playing with his quartet he carves," Mike said.

At the dinner table Kate sat and listened. The whole family, she realized, was like Mike—busy, intense, talkative, and volatile. Mrs. Gordon had marched at a peace demonstration that afternoon in front of the U.N. and was full of conversation about it; Mr. Gordon was disturbed because of a rumor that the brownstone houses on the block were to be torn down and replaced with a housing development ("Not even low-income housing," he said indignantly); and Tina, who had just been reading James Baldwin, got into a heated discussion with Mike as to whether Baldwin was a true spokesman for the Negro people or not.

"Don't mind us. We're always this way," Mike said to Kate.

"I don't mind. I'm enjoying it." And Kate was enjoying it, but she was also bewildered. Seeing Mike in his own background made her ashamed of her mother's meagre conversation and her bare, uninteresting home. Mike must have thought her family very stupid! Kate was particularly intrigued by Mrs. Gordon. If she had passed her on the street, Kate would have put her down as a rather dumpy, ordinary, simple housewife whose main involvement might be picking out the best roast for her family. She didn't look at all like the kind of woman who would march in a demonstration; Kate had always thought those women must be an odd sort, the kind who wore ill-fitting slacks and didn't comb their hair. Mrs. Gordon was feminine and motherly, her gray hair soft around her face, and she carried her plumpness with a certain grace and well-groomed style.

The atmosphere at the table was both lively and warm, and through all the talk the Gordons made Kate feel like one of them. They took her for granted in an easy, natural way, as if the family were able to stretch out readily to enclose a newcomer within its midst.

Later Kate said to Mike, "I think I could fall in love with your whole family. They're wonderful people."

"Yeah, they're okay," Mike said.

Early Saturday morning Mike and Kate went out apartment hunting for Mike. Mike wanted to be near the law school at Washington Square in Manhattan and decided that the East Village would be the best and most inexpensive place to look. "I like space," he said. "I don't want just one room. And I want to be able to cook."

He led her through a series of streets and varying neighborhoods that made Kate feel as if she were dipping into one foreign city after another. First he showed her Washington Square Park and the university buildings. Then he took her through Washington Mews, a tiny, old-fashioned cobblestone street, a remnant of old New York, standing between huge apartment buildings. "This is where I'd like to live," Kate said. "Do you think you could find an apartment here?"

Mike laughed. "People never move out of these houses, and they're fabulously expensive. You're an innocent," he said to her.

"I'm not a sophisticated New Yorker," Kate said, feeling a little hurt.

"That's what I love about you." Mike squeezed her hand. "There are thousands of sophisticated girls around, but there's only one Kate like you."

As they walked east, the neighborhood changed from

elegant to poor. East Eighth Street was a potpourri of little shops, with bizarre clothes and jewels, stuck in the basements of tenements. Farther east, where there was a mixture of Italian, Jewish, Polish, and German names, the stores were filled with the things that poor people buy: cheap housedresses, long links of sausage, old pots and cooking utensils, secondhand furniture. Kate had never seen anything like the area in her life. "It's exciting, isn't it?" Mike said. He obviously loved the crowded streets, the outdoor stalls overflowing with merchandise, the smell of the cheeses and strange foods, and the people on the sidewalk in their shabby clothes—old women with shawls on their head, young boys and girls in narrow jeans, their bare feet in sandals.

Kate didn't say anything. She wondered why people wanted to live so crowded together, when there were mountains and valleys and forests in open country. They went up and down stairs looking at dingy apartments, until Kate thought she would drop if she didn't sit down.

Mike was apologetic. He never seemed to get tired. "I'm sorry, honey, we'll go eat." Chinatown was too far to walk, so he took her to a huge delicatessen where they had hot pastrami sandwiches and coffee. They were just finishing their coffee when a tall, blond boy came over and greeted Mike.

Mike was delighted and surprised to see him, and introduced him as Gary Mitchell, an old friend of his from Brooklyn High. "What are you doing here?" Mike asked him eagerly.

Gary sat down and ordered coffee. "I live here. It's great. We have a terrific place."

"Who's we?" Mike asked.

"Me and my wife. Yeah, I'm married. We're going to have a baby any minute now." Gary looked at Kate inquiringly, and she found herself blushing.

She shook her head. "Only Mike's looking for an apartment. We're friends."

When he heard that Mike wanted a place, Gary excitedly told them that he thought there might be a vacancy in his building. "The kids upstairs are splitting up. They want to get rid of the apartment. Come on over and we can find out for sure."

"You mean they're getting divorced?" Kate's face was troubled.

"Probably. Couple of dumb kids," Gary said casually.

He led them back to his house, a tenement that looked a little cleaner than most, and up three flights of stairs to his apartment. When he opened the door, Kate was astonished. The apartment was a complete surprise. Gary had broken through a wall so that he had a good-sized living room, with clean, whitewashed walls. An old Franklin stove stood in one corner. There wasn't much furniture, but bright Indian rugs were scattered on the floor and paintings hung on the walls. "They're Mia's paintings," Gary said, introducing his wife, Mia, a serene, serious-faced girl, whose dark hair was pulled back into a pony-tail. She looked ridiculously young to be carrying a child, but Kate liked her slow smile and the way she looked at Gary when she spoke, as if she wanted his assurance that she was saying the right thing.

The boys started talking together about what Gary had done to the apartment, and Mia shyly asked Kate if she and Mike were getting married. Again Kate shook her head. "Oh, no, I'm only a sophomore at college."

Mia smiled. "I left art school to marry Gary."

"But he had finished school, hadn't he?" Kate was frankly curious.

"He had one more year of college, and then he went on to get his Master's. But he worked part-time then."

"But how did you manage? I mean—what did you live on?"

"I worked. We got along; we didn't starve. There wasn't any money for movies, or clothes, but it was all right." Mia laughed. "Sometimes we stayed up all night making Christmas cards. I went out and got a pile of orders, and Gary helped me finish them. I can't say I'm sorry it's over with. Gary has a job now." Gary was working as a draftsman in an architect's office.

Kate felt a wave of jealousy for the other girl, who was probably not more than a year or two older than herself. Mia had everything: a husband she obviously adored, a pretty apartment, a baby on the way, and her painting besides. She had a quiet self-containment, the air of a young woman who was fulfilled. The married girls that Kate knew in Vermont were always fidgeting about, emptying ashtrays, jumping up to wipe off a table, bearing the cross of their housewifely duties without a moment's let-up—but not Mia. She sat quietly and talked, and when Gary accidentally spilled some beer he was handing to Mike, she paid no attention, not even scolding him with a look. Eventually Gary cleaned it up.

"Come on," Gary said after a while, "I want to show you the apartment upstairs." He took Kate and Mike up the next flight of steps and banged on the door loudly. It was opened by a sullen-faced girl with beautifully thick hair, which looked as if it hadn't been combed in weeks. The apartment was as messy as she was. Unwashed dishes were piled high in the sink, and plates with bits of old food lay scattered about the living room. Kate tried to see the apartment behind the dirt, but it wasn't easy. She knew that if Mike moved in there she'd want to make sure it was scrubbed out with a strong antiseptic first. The living room was smaller than the Mitchells', but besides the bedroom and kitchen there was another small room that Mike said he could use as a study. He thought the arrangement was great. The rent was low, even less than what Gary paid because the apartment was on the top floor, and the rooms had plenty of light. Mike especially liked the skylight over the kitchen.

"I'll help you paint it," Gary offered.

Mike was as excited as a kid. Again Kate felt a wave of jealousy. Mike would be here with Gary and Mia downstairs, and she'd be stuck up at school taking dull courses that she wasn't truly interested in.

"You can pick up a stove like ours over on Second Avenue and hook it up to the chimney," Gary suggested. "The heat's not always too great."

"I'd like that," Mike agreed. "I have the furniture from my room at home, and I'll build some bookcases—I don't need much. I can get some stuff from the Salvation Army or the secondhand stores."

Kate remained quiet while they were busy planning. Mike turned to her suddenly. "What's the matter?"

"Nothing," she said. Mike looked at her intently, but he didn't reply.

They stopped downstairs to say good-bye to Mia, and then they walked over to the address Gary gave them for the agent of the building, so that Mike could leave a deposit and get a lease.

"Is the apartment for one or both of you?" the agent wanted to know. His question made the third time Kate had been asked if she and Mike were to be married, and it was beginning to get on her nerves. "It's just for him," she said abruptly, but her voice was sharp enough to cause Mike to look at her in surprise.

Outside, Mike took her arm in his. "What's the matter, honey? Don't say 'Nothing,' because I know something is."

"I don't know. Everyone seems to know what they want to do, except me. You have a purpose, you know where you're going. A couple like Gary and Mia, they seem to know who they are and where they're headed. Even Candy, who's kind of a nut, knows that she wants to be a chemistry major. I don't feel like going back to school." Kate said the last sentence defiantly, as if she expected Mike to argue with her.

"Then don't go back." He took her arm and held her close. "You have a place to go, a purpose—it's with me." He stood still and faced her. "Kate, why don't we get married?"

"What do you mean?" she asked illogically, feeling startled and agitated.

"I mean what I say. I mean that you, Kate Minton, and I, Mike Gordon, should get married. Now, as soon as I graduate. We can live together in that apartment. Why didn't we think of it before? You were going to come to New York this summer anyway. Why should you live alone? It would be stupid and expensive. Kate, darling, will you marry me?" Mike's eyes were sober but shining with delight and wonder at the simple perfection of what he had said.

"You mean you are proposing to me?" Kate was wide-eyed and unbelieving.

"Yes, I'm proposing to you. I think we should get married. I can't imagine why we didn't think of it before. It seems so clear and obvious and right to me now. I love you and you love me. I have to be in New York, so that's where you should be. And now we even have an apartment to live in."

"But I . . . I. . . ." she stammered helplessly.

"Don't say you have to ask your mother. You're of age—almost a year past it. Kate, darling, don't you see how right it is?"

Kate smiled. "Of course I see it. It's the rightest thing I ever heard of. I'm stunned, that's all." She looked around at the crowded, dirty street, at a man with a vending machine selling cold drinks and huge pretzels, at a raggedy little boy pulling a wagon full of groceries. "I can't believe it. That here, standing on this street corner, you would propose to me. And we could do it, couldn't we? I mean, no one could stop us—"

"No, no one could stop us." Mike leaned over and kissed her full on the mouth. "Holy smoke, but I'm excited!"

"We've got to sit down and think this out seriously," Kate said.

"I've never been more serious in my life." They walked a few blocks, holding hands and grinning at each other. Then Mike led her into a dark Italian restaurant that had beautiful artichokes and stuffed green peppers in its window. It was the middle of the afternoon and the place was completely empty; they sat down at a table with a red-

and-white-checked tablecloth. Mike ordered a small bottle of wine and some cheese and crackers.

"But what would we live on?" Kate asked.

"I'm planning to work part-time while I go to law school; a lot of the guys get jobs. My folks are going to pay my tuition anyhow and help out with my rent for a while. And you could get a job. We'd be rich. Why not, Kate? Why not? Gary and Mia did it. Millions of young people are getting married today, and we're not such kids. I'm twenty-one and you're almost nineteen. You don't really want to go back to Branston, I know. And now we have an apartment and everything."

"It scares me," Kate said. "I have to rearrange all my thinking. I had thought I'd finish college, and by that time I'd know what I wanted to do. And then later, much later, I'd get married."

"I don't believe a word of it," Mike said. "You've never really been sold on finishing college. From the first minute I met you, you said you wanted to get married and have babies. Isn't that right?"

"We certainly wouldn't have babies for a long time," Kate said emphatically.

"Not until I was earning enough money," Mike said. "I want a good-sized family. About four kids would be nice."

"Oh, Mike, we're not married yet!" Kate was laughing at his seriousness.

"You haven't said yes. Kate, will you marry me?" Their eyes met and Mike took her hand across the table.

"Yes, yes, yes. Yes, I say yes."

Mike went around the table and gave her a kiss. "I'm sorry I haven't a diamond for you," he said.

"I don't like diamonds. Mike, what's the name of this place?"

Mike looked startled. "I'll go outside and look." He came back grinning. "Tony's Restaurant. Why?"

"We've got to remember it. We've got to remember where it is. It's important; it's where we got engaged."

"And we can come back every year on this date to celebrate. I'll buy you the best dinner Tony has."

"We're grinning at each other like two idiots," Kate said, laughing. "I love you so much, Mike."

"Let's get out of here. There's something I want to do." Mike called the waiter and paid the bill.

After the darkened restaurant the bright sunshine came as a surprise. "I'd forgotten it was still afternoon," Kate said. "Are you going to tell your parents? I should call my mother, shouldn't I?"

Mike gulped. Kate had never seen him nervous before.

"I'd forgotten about our parents. I guess we do have to tell them, don't we?"

"Are you scared?"

"Sure, a little. You know what parents are like. They never think you should get married. By the way, I have a Jewish grandmother."

Kate looked surprised. "You never told me."

"I'm telling you now. She came over here because of Hitler. She's German. My mother's mother. She's great. You'll be crazy about her."

"But then isn't your mother Jewish too?"

"Half and half. My grandfather wasn't Jewish, but he hated Hitler just as much as my grandmother did. She's got some terrific stories to tell. You'll have to meet her real soon."

Kate was pensive as they walked hand in hand.

"What's the matter?" Mike glanced at her sideways. "Does it bother you that I have Jewish blood? I like it; I'm kind of proud of it. I don't know why, but I am."

"Of course, that doesn't bother me. It's just that you're so different . . . we're so different . . . our backgrounds. I'm so afraid you'll get bored with me. I feel that you give me so much more than I give you. You're exciting and I'm not. I couldn't bear it if you ever left me or fell in love with someone else. I'd want to die . . . like that girl in that apartment. She looked so miserable."

Mike put his arm around her and smoothed back her blown hair. "Darling, you're exciting to me. You're beautiful and gentle and feminine and lovely. I need you. I feel peaceful with you. It's a different kind of excitement. It's something that happens inside of me when I'm with you. As if I'm coming home."

"But people get tired of coming home." Kate's face was suddenly woebegone. "Are you sure you wouldn't rather have a girl who goes on marches and has drive and ambition?"

"Darling, I love *you*. People don't have to be alike to love each other! I need you because I'm the way I am, and you need me because you are you. We need each other precisely because we *are* different. I think we're the perfect couple."

"I hope so. Just don't ever leave me. Promise me that."

"It's the easiest promise I ever made in my life."

Mike had been leading her through a series of crooked streets, which were a mixture of factory buildings and tenements. They walked past old shops filled with copper and brassware, sweet-smelling bake shops, and down a street that displayed nothing but bridal gowns. Kate stopped at each window to examine the gowns.

"You don't want all that stuff, do you?" Mike asked. "I mean we don't need a fancy wedding, do we?"

"Not fancy. But I'd like a wedding."

"I thought we could go down to City Hall and get married."

Kate was shocked. "In a public place—I wouldn't like that. I have a little money saved. I'd like something nice."

Mike was embarrassed. "But wouldn't your mother pay for your wedding? I mean, I thought that was usual."

Kate looked unhappy. "She hasn't any money. She has a hard time just getting along. Besides," Kate added uneasily, "she might not approve."

"Will you mind terribly if she doesn't?" Mike's eyes were anxious.

"I'd like it better if she did. But"—Kate tossed her head defiantly—"she couldn't stop me. No one could."

Mike squeezed her hand. "Where do you want to get married? At home in Vermont?"

Kate's eyes were surprised. "I don't know. I've never thought about it. I mean I've thought about getting married, but I never thought about where. Do you think your parents would mind coming up to Vermont?" Kate stopped still after she asked the question. Then she shook her head vigorously. "No, it would be awful. I couldn't ask them up there." She thought of her house that now seemed so empty and colorless to her; she'd be ashamed to have people like the Gordons see it. Before Mike could say anything she continued, "I'd like Candy to be with me, to be my maid of honor."

"Well, if we have a real wedding, I'll want Jake Bernstein to stand up with me. He's a great guy, and we've been very good friends. He taught me history in high school, but he's a lawyer now, and I think he's going into politics."

"And it would be nice to invite a few of our good friends from school," Kate went on.

"Sure. Tommy, for example. And my grandmother—we couldn't leave her out. I'd like to have Gary and Mia, too. Gary's an old friend from way back, and they're in a way a little bit responsible. Seeing them gave me the courage to ask you," Mike said with a grin.

"And, of course, your sister and my brother. But where can we get married?"

"I know where. My grandmother's house!" Mike's voice was excited. "I always said I wanted to get married there. She has a marvelous old house, a brownstone, with fireplaces and tremendous rooms. She'd love it. And your mother and Judd could stay there, she'd put them up."

Kate caught his enthusiasm. "It sounds lovely. I'll take care of everything, you know, whatever work has to be done. If your grandmother likes me—"

"She'll love you. Here, this is where I want to go." Mike took Kate into a basement shop. She hardly noticed where they were going, and not until they were inside did she realize it was an antique jewelry store.

"We're looking for a ring," Mike said to the plump woman behind the counter. "Something very pretty."

The woman brought out a tray of rings, which Mike proceeded to examine.

"You're mad," Kate said. "Nutty."

"Why? Can't I buy my girl a ring?" He picked out a lovely old-fashioned gold ring with two small garnets and a pearl. "Try this one on." It fit Kate's slim finger perfectly. "Do you like it?" Mike asked.

"It's beautiful. But it's probably too expensive."

"That's my problem, not yours." The price of the ring seemed reasonable to Mike, and he bought it.

Kate was glowing. "We're engaged," she said, "really and truly engaged. I can't believe it." Every few minutes she admired her ring, with bright dewy eyes.

5

KATE SAT BETWEEN MRS.
Gordon and Mike's grandmother, Mrs. Keilwasser, listening to the Senator from Massachusetts give the graduation address. It was hot in the auditorium, and she was having a hard time keeping her eyes open. The Senator had a powerful voice, but she had heard the clichés he was mouthing so many times before: graduation was the beginning, not the end, young people have to think for themselves, have to learn not to conform, but to stand up for their beliefs. . . . And yet, Kate thought drowsily, if a student ever tried to be different, the whole world of adults jumped on him. She thought of Mike, the only person she knew who truly tried to be an independent

and original thinker, but many people, including herself, were often afraid of his ideas.

Kate felt as if she hadn't slept for weeks, and actually she had been going along with very little sleep. There had been so much to do, to think about and to talk about. She and Candy had been staying up till all hours talking about the wedding, which was to take place in four days, and before that they had been studying for finals. Kate's impulse had been not to bother with the exams, since she wasn't coming back, but Mike had persuaded her that she would be foolish to throw away a whole year of credits. He had said that she might want to finish college sometime. The possibility seemed most unlikely to her, but Mike had been so insistent that she had agreed. Certainly, she thought ruefully, she didn't have much will of her own.

Of late there had been many decisions to make, and she had been content to let Mike make most of them. When they had first told Mike's parents about their plan to get married, Mr. and Mrs. Gordon had tried to persuade Kate to finish college first. She had been touched by their concern for her, although they were frank to point out that it was closely related to their concern for Mike. "It is better for a young lawyer to have a wife with a college degree and some training for a professional career," Mrs. Gordon had said. "There are less pressures on him if he knows that his wife can, if she has to, earn a living. And," she had added, "you'd be happier too. I don't know how much you will like working at some ordinary job while Mike is still at law school—or how much he will like it, either." The Gordons had also said that they were sure her mother would object.

The more they talked, the more Mike found arguments to counter their objections. Kate had let him do the talking, thinking all the time what a fine lawyer he was going to make. She sensed that convincing them was going to be harder than convincing her mother. Kate didn't think that her mother cared very much whether or not she finished college. She wouldn't have been surprised if Mrs. Minton admitted she thought it was rather a waste of time, although she did enjoy telling her friends and the other teachers at school that her daughter was at Branston U.

The whole discussion had ended up with Mike stating flatly that he knew he was doing the right thing in getting married and that he wanted to take no chance of losing Kate. Once the Gordons realized that nothing they said would change Mike's mind, they gave in gracefully to the situation. Tina was the most excited. "Will you have a real wedding, with a train and a long veil? Can I be a brides-maid? I could wear a pale blue satin gown and carry a little bouquet of yellow roses—"

"I don't think Kate is going to want a very big wed-ding," Mrs. Gordon said. "I'm sure she'll want to talk it over with her mother before she decides anything."

As it happened, Kate depended more on Mrs. Gordon and on Mike for help and advice than she did on her mother. Mrs. Minton wept when Kate told her that she wanted to get married, and she kept saying over and over again how bad she felt that she couldn't afford to give Kate a beautiful big wedding. Actually she was quite re-lieved when Kate told her that it would be more practical for them to get married in New York, and she quickly assumed that Mike came from a very rich family. This notion completely satisfied her doubts about Kate's leav-ing college. At home for a weekend, Kate had been aston-ished to hear her mother telling all her friends that Kate was marrying a rich boy from New York, that they were giving her a wedding, and that Kate didn't really have to finish college because she'd never have to work. When Kate told her mother that she was going to have to find a job right away and work while Mike went to law school, Mrs. Minton said she thought it was a very nice thing for

Kate to do, and that Mike was a lucky boy to have a girl who wouldn't squander his money. Nothing Kate said could get the idea out of her mother's head.

After the graduation Kate went down to New York with the Gordons and Tante Sara, the name Mrs. Keilwasser had always been called. Mike remained at school to take care of a few things, and Kate was to stay with Tante Sara until the wedding.

Tante Sara's house was exactly as Mike had described it—an old-fashioned brownstone with big, high-ceilinged rooms filled with heavy mahogany furniture and crystal chandeliers and, to Kate's delight, wood-burning fireplaces. Tante Sara herself was a tiny woman, with white hair and wide-set young eyes, who moved and walked like a girl. Kate fell quite in love with her and was very happy that she was being married in her house.

"I hate to do this to a bride," Tante Sara said, when they got home, "but I'm going to put you to work."

Kate was more than willing, and together she and Mrs. Keilwasser polished drawer after drawer of silver, punch bowls, and coffee sets; they washed dishes and polished already shining tabletops. Mrs. Keilwasser had a maid who washed the windows and scrubbed the floors. "For a wedding, everything must be just right," Tante Sara said.

That evening Kate's muscles ached, but Tante Sara seemed as fresh as ever. "You are marrying a very tough young man," she said to Kate at the dinner table. "He is stubborn like his grandfather. You will have to work around his stubbornness."

"What do you mean by that?" Kate asked.

"You cannot budge men like my husband. Once they make up their mind to something, they don't change. My husband, John, risked his life over and over again to save many Jews while we were still in Germany. Often I was frightened and I thought he did too much. But nothing would stop him, not even the first warning he had with his heart. The strain was too much for him and it killed him. Mike is like that. You will have to watch him, but very subtly so that he doesn't even know you are taking care of him. And sometimes you will have to sit quietly and say nothing while you know he is endangering himself. It is not easy."

"Is that what you did?" Kate asked. "Did you sit by quietly and watch?"

Tante Sara smiled. "I'm afraid not. Sometimes I risked my life with him; other times I made great scenes, begging him to stay at home with me. But I never won." Her lips were still smiling, but her eyes were sad. "I hurt us both with my scenes."

"I know what you mean about Mike," Kate said thoughtfully. "He'll fight to the death for what he believes in. But I'm not like you. I don't know that I could fight alongside him or that I could even make a scene. I'd just be miserable, alone."

"That's the worse thing you can do." Tante Sara drew her tiny self up tall. "A woman has to go along with her man as much as she can, but if she doesn't agree with him she has to speak. Too many women cry out their anguish alone and accomplish nothing."

Kate felt that she was being given valuable advice, but at the same time it didn't touch her. She knew that she would never be alone once she was married to Mike and that they would be able to discuss any differences between them.

Kate lay in the big four-poster bed in Tante Sara's house. She could hear her mother, who had arrived the day before, moving in the next room. Judd was already downstairs having breakfast; she had heard him clumping heavily down the steps. Today was her wedding day.

The sun came through the slats of the Venetian blinds in slanted stripes, making weird patterns on the floor and on the chair where she had dropped her clothes the night before. Looking around the room, Kate felt that nothing could possibly down her spirits. The past few days she had moved in a world that was so marvelously new and exciting she wondered how she had ever survived her old, drab existence.

Tante Sara's energy and gaiety had been infectious. She turned everything she did into an entertainment, and as she and Mrs. Gordon had taken Kate around New York— to buy a bed for their apartment, to select a hi-fi set, Tante Sara's wedding gift, off to a hairdresser for Kate, out to lunch—Kate felt that not only was she marrying Mike, she was becoming part of a family that was warm and giving. She couldn't quite believe that besides having Mike she was acquiring all these new relatives, too.

Kate got out of bed, slipped on a robe, and went downstairs for breakfast. Her mother was there by this time, and Kate joined the others in the kitchen.

"Happy wedding day." Tante Sara came over and kissed her.

"Yes, happy wedding day," Mrs. Minton echoed, and kissed her daughter too. She held Kate off at arm's length and studied her face. "I hope you are doing the right thing, my dear, I only hope so. It's very hard being a mother when there is no father. I always depended so on my husband," she explained to Tante Sara.

"It's too late now, Mom," Judd said cheerfully. "Stop worrying, will you?"

Kate gave him a grateful look. Striking an unpleasant note was typical of her mother, but even that, Kate was determined, would not bother her today.

"We're going to be fine, Mom, please don't worry about us," Kate said. "I'm starved. The smells in this kitchen are divine."

Trays of cookies were cooling on the counter, and a huge turkey was roasting in the oven. The wedding was to be a simple one at noon, with Mike's family, including a few aunts and uncles, Mrs. Minton and Judd, and some of Mike's and Kate's friends. After the ceremony they were serving a buffet luncheon. Kate had insisted on buying champagne as well as most of the food, but both Mrs. Gordon and Tante Sara were adding their own extras. Mrs. Minton had wept again about the fact that she couldn't give her daughter a "real wedding," but Kate had assured her that she was having exactly the kind of wedding she wanted and that she didn't want her mother, with her meagre income, to be burdened with anything.

"I'm glad to see a bride eat a hearty breakfast," Tante Sara commented. "It's a good way to start."

"Why shouldn't I eat? I'm so happy," Kate said.

After a while Mrs. Minton went upstairs with Kate to help her dress. Kate had bought her dress, weeks before, in Boston. Now she looked at the pale blue satin sheath critically. Suddenly it looked too simple and defenseless. "Do you think it's all right, Mom?"

"Why didn't you get white?" Mrs. Minton asked.

Kate ignored the question. White would have seemed too corny to her, but she couldn't explain that to her mother. She was overcome by a sudden wave of nervousness. "Oh, Mom. . . ." She held back the words, *I'm scared* —her mother wouldn't understand. No more than Mrs. Minton would respond to Kate's sudden yearning for her mother to take her in her arms and cuddle her. All these other people, the Gordons and Tante Sara, were nice, but they were really strangers. How could she live among them, adapt to their ways—to Mike's ways?

"Mary Louise had a beautiful white gown and a veil of real lace. For her, and you know she's not the prettiest girl, she looked real nice. Her bridesmaids wore yellow. There were two of them, the Titcomb girls, her cousins, and of course they're both too fat, but they didn't look bad. Not bad at all."

For once Kate was grateful for her mother's chatter. The wild panic slowly subsided, lulled by the accompaniment of the familiar stream of words, and Kate looked at her mother's tired, wispy face with affection. "You're incredible, Mom," she said, impulsively giving her mother a vigorous hug.

"My goodness, you're so strong, Kate. You know Miss Pettit, the little dressmaker, remember she lives on Grove Street. One of her customers hugged her and broke her rib. She had trouble breathing for weeks, poor thing."

Kate giggled. "Mom, you really are incredible."

"I now pronounce you man and wife."

Kate had been listening intently to every word of Judge Sullivan's marriage service. Oblivious of everyone else, she had felt that the Judge was speaking only to Mike and her. When Mike had vetoed a religious ceremony—"I'm not a church-goer," he had said, "and I see no reason to change now"—she had been disappointed. But Judge Sullivan, an old friend of the Gordons', had given them a ceremony that Kate thought was the most beautiful she had ever heard.

Then, when Mike turned to kiss her, she knew that this moment was the most important and moving one in her life. The old lovers' litany, "Love like ours will never die," was burning in her head, and as she gently touched the wedding ring on her finger she felt as if she were floating off into a promised world where happiness was an accepted way of life.

The rest of the wedding would remain a hazy memory. Candy, her maid of honor, said, "I always knew you'd get married first." Kate was aware that someone played Tante Sara's fine old Steinway grand, that at some point she and Mike cut a high, tiered, white wedding cake (who had thought to order it?), that a pile of magnificently wrapped wedding presents were stacked up on a table, that many people kissed her, and that Mrs. Gordon had whispered to her, "I think you and Mike should start on your way before it gets too late."

She also knew that each time she looked at Mike she couldn't quite believe that this strong, animated, laughing boy was to be part of her life forever after.

Kate's sigh was one of weary but wonderfully happy relief as she and Mike drove away in the car Mr. Gordon had lent them. They were headed for Sag Harbor, where they would spend a three-day honeymoon in a cottage that Jake Bernstein, Mike's best man, had managed to get for them from a friend. Three whole beautiful days, Kate thought, closing her eyes to the ugliness of Long Island City as Mike maneuvered the car through traffic. She wasn't counting today, Saturday, because that was almost over, but they'd have Sunday, Monday, and Tuesday. They didn't have to get home until Tuesday evening, in time for Mike to start classes on Wednesday. The weather prediction had been sunny and warm. . . .

"Are you tired, darling?" Mike pulled her over closer to him.

"Not really. Just happy. Happy thinking about the next three days. Walking on the beach, swimming, having nothing to do except be with you."

"I've been wanting to talk to you about that, but it seems to me we haven't had a minute alone for days and days. Would you mind terribly if we came in early Tuesday afternoon instead of Tuesday night?"

"Why should we do that? I mean if it's warm and sunny, why not stay out there? We have so little time."

Mike didn't answer while he slowed down for a traffic light. His eyes were glued on the light, waiting for it to change.

"Why should we go in early?" Kate repeated her question.

"Well, it's not too important. It's just that there's a peace demonstration I thought we might go to. It's for five o'clock Tuesday. I thought it might be fun for you."

"Oh, Mike!" Kate looked at him and laughed. There was something so lovable about the way he was pretending to be offhand, but she also felt a pang of fear. "You mean you want to go. Why don't you say so?"

"It's not that important. I can stop and send Jake a wire—"

"You mean you already told him we were coming?" Kate's eyes were on him.

"I said we'd try to be there. Forget it, honey, it doesn't matter."

"But it does matter, Mike." Kate's voice was grave. "You want to go, and you should say so. We have to be square with each other, right from the beginning."

"Honey, don't make a thing out of it. I only thought it would be fun. A lot of the kids will be there, and we could all go out to supper together someplace afterwards. Also I thought you might want a little more time getting settled in Tuesday night. I'd hate to leave you Wednesday with all the unpacking."

"You've really thought it all out. You want to go very much. I think we should go then."

"But you don't want to, do you?"

"I thought we were on our honeymoon," Kate said wistfully.

"Now you've made a whole thing out of nothing. Please, honey, let's forget it." Mike pulled up the car to a public telephone booth. "Jake's probably still at Tante Sara's. I'll send him a wire." He made a move to get out of the car, but Kate put her hand on his arm.

"Mike, please don't call. Let's go."

"Only if you really want to." His eyes met hers.

"I want to because you do."

"And you won't be mad on Tuesday if it's a gorgeous day and we have to leave early?"

Kate laughed. "Think how awful I'd feel if it rained and you'd said we weren't coming."

Mike moved the car back into the stream of traffic, and they drove on. Kate closed her eyes again to rest, but she didn't feel quite as completely at peace with herself and the world as she had when the honeymoon began.

6

THE FIRST SUNDAY THAT Kate and Mike were in their new apartment, Kate invited Gary and Mia up for Sunday breakfast. "The place is a mess," Kate said, waving at the unpacked cartons of books and the pictures stacked against the wall, "but if I waited until everything was done, it might be years before you came up."

"Don't worry," Gary said soothingly, "Mike and I will get to those bookshelves this afternoon."

"But Mike didn't get the lumber." There was a note of accusation in Kate's voice.

Mike laughed. "Of course not, honey. We have to figure out where we're going to put the shelves, and then measure how much wood we need. It's not a big production, but it all takes time. You can't put up bookshelves one, two, three."

"But you have to start," Kate murmured.

Kate served them an excellent breakfast of country sausage and crisp French toast with maple syrup. "She even makes great coffee," Mike said proudly.

"She's a good cook," Gary agreed.

"She's a good everything." Mike leaned over and kissed Kate. "Let's go downstairs and take a look at the ball game on your TV set before we get to work," he suggested to Gary.

"That's the end of them," Mia said good-naturedly, when the boys left. She had her baby beside her in a small portable carriage.

"You mean they won't come back to measure for the bookshelves?" Kate was indignant.

"Not if I know Gary. Once he starts watching the ball game, that's the end."

"Don't you care?"

Mia shrugged her shoulders. "He loves it. What can I do?"

"Well, I care," Kate said. "I hate living in a mess, and Mike promised he'd get started. I have to go out and look for a job tomorrow."

Mia's eyes were sympathetic. "It's too bad you can't wait a few weeks until you get settled."

"We can't afford it. We're practically at the bottom of our savings now. That's why I'd like to get as much of the apartment finished as we can, while we still have a little money left. Otherwise it'll get eaten up."

"Wouldn't it be better to save it until you get a job?"

"I'll get a job. I have to," Kate said confidently. "I'd rather have the bookshelves and eat beans anyway," she added.

Mia was right. It was almost four o'clock when the boys came back, and no sooner did they come in than Jake Bernstein arrived with a group of friends. Kate knew it was the end of the bookshelves for that day.

Jake brought two law students who were taking courses with Mike, and a very pretty girl, Peggy Cannon, who was working for her Master's in sociology. "We've got a problem," Jake announced, "and we want your help. All of you," he said, addressing Kate and Mike and the Mitchells. "We've got a chance of electing a really good man to Congress this November, Paul O'Donnell, but it's going to take a lot of work. We need people to address envelopes and stuff them, we need typing, and most of all we need people to go out and ring doorbells and talk to everyone about Paul. He's a great guy, he really is—he's on our side on civil rights, on foreign policy, and on the local anti-poverty program, which we badly need in this neighborhood."

"You don't have to sell me," Mike said fervently. "I've heard about O'Donnell, and I'll do everything I can to help elect him."

Kate was pouring coffee for everyone. "You'll be pretty busy with school and studying," she murmured.

"I know, but I'll still have time in the evenings and weekends. Count me in," he said to Jake.

Gary and Mia promised to help too. "I can address envelopes while I'm home with the baby," Mia said.

"And what about you?" Jake turned to Kate.

"I'll have my job. Between that and taking care of the house, cooking, and marketing, I don't think I'll have much time."

"You could ring a few doorbells," Mike said gently.

"Oh, no, I couldn't do that." Kate looked uncomfortable and glanced at Mike appealingly.

"She's shy," Mike said, patting her. No one urged her, but Kate felt an awkward silence for a few seconds until the conversation started up again.

Jake and his two law-student friends, Russ and Walter,

went out and brought back pizza for everyone. Kate put on another pot of coffee and felt that that was what she had been doing all day. She hadn't even been out of the house, although she had been looking forward to taking a walk around the neighborhood with Mike. It was after nine when the group broke up and everyone went home.

Kate sank down on a chair, tired out. "It was a nice day, wasn't it?" Mike said, sitting down opposite her. "Come over here. You're too far away."

When Kate didn't answer or move, Mike looked at her inquiringly. "What's the matter, honey? You tired?"

"Uh-huh."

"Come sit by me. I'll rub your back."

"I'm all right over here," Kate said.

"What's the matter? What's wrong? I suppose you're mad because I didn't get to the bookshelves." Mike sighed despondently. "I'm sorry. But I got so excited about this election campaign. It'll be terrific if we get O'Donnell in. I've never worked in an election before. I think it'll be fun."

"Especially with a pretty girl like Peggy Cannon," Kate remarked. She knew the remark was stupid, but it slipped out.

"Is she pretty? I didn't notice. Kate, darling, please don't be silly."

"I'm not silly," Kate said unconvincingly. "Just tired."

Mike came over and took her in his arms. "I love you, Kate. Don't forget that."

"And I love you." Kate held on to him tightly. "I guess I just wish you were a little different in some ways. I feel as if I hadn't seen you all day."

"You don't want us to stay here and only look at each other, do you?"

"It might be nice," she said softly. She did love him, and she was proud of him, yet she had felt cut off from him this day. If he worked evenings in the election campaign, they'd have even less time together. And would he be able to fit in a part-time job? Though they hadn't discussed it for some weeks, Kate had assumed Mike was still planning to work. But she didn't want to ask him, not now.

She had thought when she married Mike she would never feel alone again, and she clung to him, wishing she could escape that exact feeling now.

The woman with the blue-white hair at the employment agency was harried and brusque. She spoke in unfinished sentences, and her desk was littered with scribbled notes and index cards. During the week she had sent Kate out on several interviews, but so far no job had materialized.

"College graduates, college graduates, that's all they want. Why didn't you finish college?" she demanded of Kate accusingly.

"I told you. I left to get married. That's why I need a job. My husband is going to law school."

"He should be the one to—oh, well, it's none of my business. Go to this place. It's not great, but—oh, dear, I hope this is the right address. Nice people, very nice people. Call me up later this afternoon."

Kate took the card handed to her, went through the outer office hurriedly, preferring not to see the pale faces of the others seeking jobs, and emerged into the glaring Fifth Avenue sunshine. She had never spent a summer in the city before and she found the heat unbearably oppressive. For a moment she closed her eyes and thought of her hammock under the shade trees in Vermont. What was she doing in New York in June, trying to get a crummy office job? The people rushing past her looked preoccupied and unhappy, as if they too knew the city was a foolish place to be on a burning summer's day. Kate felt trapped with them, caught up in a life that was not of her choosing.

But I *did* choose it, she thought to herself, falling in step with the crowd. I chose to marry Mike and to get a job and live in New York. She drew herself up, taking a certain pride in her decision, as if wanting to convince herself that the hardships were a valuable part of the scheme.

The woman from the employment agency had been right—it wasn't a great job—but the two brothers who ran the small import office appeared agreeable enough and offered Kate the position. She was to do typing, filing, and answering the telephone. Kate accepted the job promptly.

That afternoon, when she went home through the jumbled East Side streets, she had a feeling of elation and a sense of belonging to the city that she had not felt since she had come to New York. "Isn't it a beautiful day?" She had a warm smile for the tired Italian vegetable man, sitting under the awning of his store, wearing a neatly patched old brown sweater.

"Too hot, too hot," he muttered.

"Why don't you take off your sweater?" Kate was slightly bewildered by the absurdity of the heavy piece of clothing.

"Make no difference. I wear this sweater winter, summer. Make no difference."

The people in the Puerto Rican grocery store, the Jewish butcher—Kate wanted to tell them all that she had a job and that she was going to be a real New Yorker, riding in the subway, rushing on the streets like everyone else. Mike wasn't home yet when she got there, and she went downstairs to tell Mia her news.

"It's not much of a job, but it's a job. I splurged and bought a bottle of wine and a teeny steak. I'm really very pleased about it," Kate said, after telling Mia what the job was.

"I think it's great," Mia said, but her face was thoughtful and reserved.

"What's the matter? Don't you think I should have taken it?"

"I don't know. I guess I can't see you sitting in some dingy office doing typing and answering the telephone. You're too good for that."

"No one else seems to think so. Everyone wants college graduates. I have no special talents, and I'm not ambitious. I want to be Mike's wife, that's all," Kate added in a serious vein.

"I hope that'll be enough," Mia said, looking evasive.

"Isn't being Gary's wife enough for you?"

"Not entirely," Mia confessed. "I have the baby, and I

do some community work, but most important of all I have my painting. I don't think I could exist without that. It's a part of me that's mine alone, that no one, not even Gary, can touch. I don't think any intelligent woman today can find total fulfillment in being somebody's wife. I don't mean that every woman has to have a career—don't misunderstand me. I don't care what she has, whether it's playing the piano, writing sonnets, or even making clothes, but she has to have something of her own that gives her satisfaction, that she can turn to when the going gets rough. Something that has nothing to do with her husband."

"Well, I'll have my little old job," Kate said laughingly. She knew that Mike and his enthusiasms were more than enough to fill her life.

When Mike came home, Kate had the table set with her best cloth along with candles and a small bunch of flowers she had bought from a pushcart.

"Something good happen today, honey?" Mike asked, kissing her.

"I've got a job!" Kate quickly told him what it was. She was astonished, however, to find that Mike's reaction was similar to Mia's, except that Mike was far more outspoken.

"It doesn't sound to me like anything to celebrate. I

don't want you working in some creep's office doing typing. It's ridiculous. I think you ought to turn it down and wait until something decent comes along."

"But nothing decent will. I've had a slew of interviews this week. Everyone wants a college graduate for the really good jobs. I'm perfectly happy with it," Kate said, beginning to feel a little put out. "I don't know why you should object."

"Because I don't think you'll be happy with it for long. Besides, you're my wife, and you're beautiful and intelligent and you should be doing something more interesting than that." Mike was trying to win her over, but his words only made her more irritated.

"Everyone doesn't have to do something *interesting!* I'm just plain me. And you forget one little item—money. We're practically cleaned out."

"We won't go hungry. I can always borrow from my folks until you get a job."

"But I don't want to borrow from your folks! Did that ever occur to you? I'd rather scrub floors than start off getting into debt."

"Oh, Kate, for heaven's sake. Going into debt is no crime. Please don't turn into a martyr. I hate martyrs."

"I came home all excited because I had a job, and I

thought you'd be glad, too. Now you say you hate me."
Kate was close to tears.

"I didn't say I hated you, darling." Mike put his arms
around her. "I just said I hated martyrs. If you want the
job, all right. I only thought you were grabbing the first
thing too hurriedly, that's all."

"You wouldn't think I was grabbing the first thing if
you'd been going around all week the way I have," Kate
said, sobbing.

Mike soothed her and patted her until she stopped crying. "Now let's eat whatever delicious meal you're about
to give me," Mike said. "I'm starved. I have to go to a
meeting later," he added casually.

Kate looked up sharply. "What kind of a meeting?"

"About this election campaign. I won't be long. You can
come if you want to," he said.

"I thought we'd have a nice evening at home together,
just you and me. I thought it would be kind of a celebra-
tion, for my job, that is," she said ruefully.

"I didn't know about your job, honey, and I couldn't
have changed this meeting even if I had. I won't be gone
more than an hour."

Kate didn't say anything more, but after dinner when
Mike left she felt an overwhelming depression. Maybe she

should have gone to the meeting with him, but meetings bored her. She walked around the apartment restlessly, and then pulled a chair up to the open windows. It was a hot night and the street was filled with old women sitting on camp stools, children running around, and teen-agers playing their flirting games. Kate wondered what secrets those old-world women knew about love and marriage. Had they kept a small, private niche for themselves, as Mia had advised?

She got up again. And while washing up the supper dishes, emptying the ash trays, straightening a chair, running a dustcloth over a table, she was trying to understand her dream of a perfect union. Did a husband and wife exist who were at one with each other, holding nothing back, merging their lives without effort? Kate was frightened for herself and Mike, afraid of the wide gap between reality and the way she had imagined they would be. It was impossible to know whether she or Mike was the one who was out of step. She loved Mike so much, but was that the total answer?

When Kate walked by the cartons of books, still unpacked, she gave them a vicious kick.

7

KATE WASN'T AT ACE IM-
port Company for more than a week before she knew she
hated her job. The two Gabriel brothers, Mr. Larry and
Mr. Victor, were very nice, but they were rarely there. Kate
sat by herself in a tiny office typing out order slips, answering the telephone, and drinking coffee to keep herself from
falling asleep. To save money she brought her lunch with
her, so she didn't even have the diversion of a lunch out,
and besides, as she said to Mike, she'd have no one to eat
with anyway. Since ten minutes was enough to eat her
sandwich and drink her thermos of milk, she forced herself
to go out for a twenty-minute walk, but the neighborhood
was crowded and dull, and the streets were stiflingly hot.

As the weeks went on Kate felt herself caught up in a

deadly routine of getting up in the morning, fighting the subway rush, counting through the hours of the long day, marketing, and coming home to cook dinner for herself and Mike. The worst of it was that she was too proud and stubborn to admit to Mike how much she loathed the job—perhaps he had been right in telling her not to take it, but how soon would she have landed another? And what would they have done about money? She felt strongly about not wanting to borrow, and the whole vicious circle made her irritable.

Worst of all was getting up in the morning when Mike was still in bed. Most of his courses were in the afternoon, and he stayed up late either studying or going to one of his meetings. One morning, instead of tiptoeing around as she usually did in order not to wake Mike, she let her annoyance get the best of her and she made a big clatter.

Mike sat up in bed. "What's going on? What's the matter? Can't a guy sleep around here?"

"It's no fun having breakfast alone every day," Kate said grumpily. "Watching you sleep."

"Why didn't you say so?" Mike jumped out of bed, but he looked so sleepy and dazed that Kate felt contrite.

"Don't get up, darling. Go back to bed. I'm sorry. I'm just in a bad mood this morning."

"Then I'll make breakfast. You sit down and relax."

"Oh, would you, Mike? Then I'll try to do something with my hair for a change. I've been going around looking like a fright."

"You're beautiful," Mike said absently. He was struggling to get the eggs out of the refrigerator. "Why do you keep the eggs way in the back?" He took out several bowls of leftovers from last night's dinner. "This is the most disorganized icebox!"

"I told you to go back to bed," Kate called from the bathroom, where she was fussing with her hair.

"Oh, damn!"

Kate heard a crash and a plop. Mike had dropped a bowl of eggs on the floor. He was standing in his pajamas and bare feet swearing at the mess. "Why do you put the eggs in a bowl? Why can't you leave them in the box? How should I know there were eggs in this bowl?"

"Well, you're a great help. The one morning you get up, all you do is yell at me, criticize everything I do, and make a big mess. Your own mother said it was a shame I had to work so hard, but you don't care. You think it's fine that you're going to school, having a great time, while I sit in a crummy office all day."

Mike was trying to clean up the mess. "I don't like it any more than you do. Do you think I enjoy having you earn the money while I'm still in school? But it's just for this year and next. And if you weren't so stubborn you'd try to find a better job—one that you liked, at least."

"You go out and find me a better job and I'll take it," Kate said tartly. She was busy fixing her lunch. "I'll get a cup of coffee uptown," she said at the door.

"Don't go off mad." Mike held her back and tried to kiss her.

"But I am mad. I can't help it. I have to go. I'm late." She let him kiss her on the check, but she ran out without kissing him back.

As usual when Kate had a run-in with Mike, she felt sorry immediately afterward. Today, however, she was more displeased with herself than with Mike, and she was aware that her own frustrations were at the heart of her troubles. Mike was right. She had known when they got married that she'd have to work while Mike went to school, but the idea had seemed rather fascinating and easy to her. Now the reality of this deadly job was too much. She felt she was being a poor sport about it—but she was the one who had to watch the money, who had to scrimp at marketing, while Mike seemed to be enjoying his life much more. And he had forgotten all about trying to get a part-time job.

There seemed no way out of the dilemma. She was doing everything for Mike—working, housekeeping, cooking, worrying about money—because she loved him, but for those very same reasons she was turning into a grumpy, unlovely girl. Kate vowed to turn over a new leaf that very day. She'd be gay, she'd see to it that she and Mike had fun together, she wouldn't complain, she'd forget about the bookcases. What harm did the cartons do? If Mike didn't care, why should she?

With her new resolution very much in mind, Kate decided to be thoroughly impractical. On the way home from work she took the money she had been saving for the utility bill and bought a new record, some expensive tobacco for Mike's pipe, and a rich Italian dessert that Mike loved, but which was usually beyond their budget.

She came home, with her peace offerings, to find a houseful. Although taken by surprise, she determinedly refused to let her mind dwell on her fatigue after the hot, dreary day in the office. She would be a good sport and join in the gaiety.

Mike's face was apprehensive. "Hope you don't mind that the gang came up. You won't have to cook dinner," he added hurriedly. "Peggy's making some spaghetti." Kate then spied Peggy Cannon in her kitchen, very suntanned and pretty, surrounded by half the pots and kitchen utensils Kate owned.

"Mike, honey, where's the oregano?" Peggy called.

Kate's face froze. "I don't like strangers in my kitchen," she said in a tight voice.

"Peg's no stranger. She's a friend," Mike said. "I'll get the oregano. It's on the top shelf." He went into the kitchen.

Kate took her presents into the bedroom and dumped them on the bed. Looking at them made her want to cry. She stayed in the bedroom, trying desperately to control herself. She didn't want to be a spoilsport, she didn't want to be a nagging wife, but why did Mike have to bring that girl around, and into her kitchen? She tried to be sensible and logical: she had nothing against Peggy, she actually hardly knew her, but right now she hated her intensely, because she was gay and pretty and tan and getting her sociology Master's on top of that.

"What are you doing?" Mike stuck his head in the door.

"I'll be out in a few minutes," Kate said, without turning around. She didn't want Mike to see her unhappy face. "I want to get out of these clothes."

"Hurry up," Mike said.

Kate took off her street clothes and put on a pair of shorts and a cool, sleeveless blouse. Looking in the mirror she hated herself even more. Her legs and arms were white. In the summer she was used to being suntanned, but this summer there had been no long, lazy days in the sun.

When she joined the others she noticed that everyone, even Mike, looked brown. "Where have you all been?" Kate asked curiously. "You all look tan."

Mike grinned. "We cut classes this afternoon and went to the beach. It was too hot. I thought of calling you up and telling you to say you had a headache and leave, but I knew you wouldn't do it."

"You went to the beach!" Kate was stunned. Mike had cut classes and gone to the beach, while she had been sweating it out in a stinky office in order to *send* him to those classes. The fact that he knew she was too conscientious to leave infuriated her even more. That was the straw that broke the camel's back.

She didn't want to be conscientious and responsible; she wanted to be carefree and gay. She didn't want to support a household. The situation was completely out of control —beyond any semblance of her idea of a happy marriage.

Mike looked at her helplessly as she stood there immobilized. She could hear the voices around her, engaged in a heated discussion on a point of law, Peggy throwing in her comments from the open kitchen. To Kate they seemed to be speaking in a foreign language. The exclusion was more than she could bear. Without a word she turned her back to Mike and went into the bedroom. She pulled a skirt out of the closet and wrapped it around her shorts; she didn't like seeing girls in shorts on a city street.

Her presents for Mike, still unopened on the bed, looked more forlorn than ever. The Italian dessert would spoil, but she didn't care. One tiny piece of luck was with her, for she saw Mike go into the bathroom. She could leave quickly now, before he came out, and avoid a scene in front of all his friends. Kate grabbed her handbag and slipped out the front door.

She walked, heading west. She walked and walked, not caring where she went, not noticing what streets she was passing. Once she thought she was in front of the antique shop where Mike had bought her ring. She wasn't absolutely sure it was the same one, but it resembled it closely enough to bring tears to her eyes as she gazed at the display of old rings in the window. What had happened, what had happened?

Mike hadn't changed. He was the same intense, excited boy she had fallen in love with—and still loved. Had she changed, or had she always been jealous, sorry for herself, and resentful? It didn't seem so to her. She had certainly felt inadequate many times in the past, especially with intellectuals like Mike's friends, but she felt she had at least had a happy disposition. She and Candy, who was very different from her, had been congenial. Those long talks and giggles with Candy now were like something out of a distant, young past. It seemed impossible to Kate that she was only nineteen years old. The young college girl had stepped into the combined role of wage-earner, wife, housemaid, cook and bookkeeper, and she was unprepared. She didn't know how to follow all the rules that were prescribed for "holding a man": to be gracious and amusing at the end of the day, always to look attractive, even early in the morning, to be a good and willing listener, to talk about a husband's work—some nights she was too tired to do anything, even listen, and Mike was so busy it was hard to keep up—to be a charming hostess to his friends. She flunked on all counts.

Kate felt terribly alone as she walked up one street and down another in the summer twilight. She wondered what Mike was thinking, what he was doing. Maybe he was out looking for her. She wanted to turn around and run back to him, to have him take her in his arms and comfort her, hold her tight and tell her that he loved her, but when she thought of Peggy Cannon cooking in her kitchen, of Mike going to the beach, she walked on.

If only she had Candy, or someone close to talk to. Then on an inspiration she went down into the subway. She could go out to Tante Sara's house. She knew Tante Sara would be home—she hardly ever went out in the evening—and Kate felt that spilling out their private problems to her would not be disloyal to Mike. Tante Sara loved Mike, and maybe she could help.

Tante Sara was in her large basement kitchen baking when Kate arrived. "It's too hot in the daytime," she explained. "These are for the Community Center. They're having a food sale." The row of fresh fruit pies and the tins of cookies just out of the oven made the kitchen smell marvelous. Seeing Tante Sara, tiny, erect, and gay in a bright orange apron, immediately made Kate feel that she had come to the right place. If anyone did, this young-old woman would know the secrets of love and marriage. She would have answers to the problems troubling Kate.

"Here, have some nice cold milk and cookies." Tante Sara filled a glass for Kate and piled cookies on a plate.

Kate realized she hadn't had any supper, and she ate and drank gratefully. "Aren't you going to ask me why I'm here?" she asked.

"When you're ready you'll tell me. I didn't think you just happened to be passing by out here in Brooklyn," Tante Sara said drily. "You had a fight with your husband, probably."

"Not exactly a fight. I walked out."

"Does he know you're here?"

Kate shook her head. "He doesn't know where I am. There were a lot of people in the house, and I left while he was in the bathroom."

"You want him to worry about you?" The old woman looked at Kate shrewdly.

Kate smiled. "That's not why I left, not to make him worry."

"Don't you think I'd better call him and tell him where you are?" Tante Sara was going on with her work of gently removing the cookies from their tins.

"Let him worry a bit. You can call him a little later. I—I hardly know how to start. It's not that Mike and I fight. We do a little, but it's mainly me. I'm a terrible wife and I'm disgusted with myself." Kate nibbled on another cookie.

"You think you're a terrible wife, or Mike thinks so?"

"He doesn't say so, but I'm sure he must. I never used to complain, but now it seems that's all I do. I'm not happy, so how can I make him happy? I hate my job, I resent working, marketing, cooking, worrying about money. While Mike, well, today he cut classes and went to the beach. That burned me up. He's having a ball going to school, he's busy with this election campaign, he's having a full, wonderful time while I feel like a dumb drudge."

"I didn't think going to law school was such a ball," Tante Sara said thoughtfully. "I thought it was very hard work. And the election campaign—it's not as if he was going to parties or was out with another girl."

"There is a girl. She's part of his gang. I'm not worried about her, but I'm jealous of her anyway. She's interested in the same things he is, she's free and fun . . . I hate her." Kate looked up at Tante Sara with miserable eyes.

Tante Sara shook her head. "For such a pretty and intelligent girl," she said, "how can you get yourself in such a state of mind? You want to be someone you are not, and you don't appreciate what you are. Mike has more sense than you have. He loves you because you have character, and you want to throw it away because you don't have some kind of dazzling personality."

Kate made a grimace. "Character! I haven't even got that, because I don't *want* to be good and reliable. That sounds dull to me."

"It's dull if you make it dull. It wasn't dull of you to break away from that little village in Vermont, to get a scholarship, to fall in love with Mike and get married, to come to New York and get a job. To be helping Mike through law school and running a house. How many girls can do all that?"

"Lots of girls get married to students and go to work. I'm not the only one."

Tante Sara shrugged. "So they have worries too. The trouble today is everybody has to be somebody big and important. When I was a girl no one told us we were stupid if we stayed home and did the baking and the sewing and maybe played the piano a little bit. But today a girl does that and everyone screams at her that she's a dope."

"Everything's different now. We can't go back to the 'old days,' and girls like me who have no ambition are stuck. We're neither here nor there. I thought marrying Mike would be everything, but I feel trapped. Caught in a groove of chores and a dumb job."

"I know, I know. Let me tell you something. Women

are crazy, every one of us. We tell our children love and marriage are beautiful, everything a woman needs. But any married woman can tell you that just having a husband isn't enough. It never was. Every woman has to have something, a little corner of her own." Tante Sara looked at Kate with sympathetic eyes. "Mike is a wonderful boy, but he's got a big ego; he knows what he wants and he'll go after it. He'll leave you behind if you don't make something for yourself—any really interesting man will."

"I know," Kate said, her lips trembling. "That's what I'm afraid of. I don't know what to do."

"Here, take some more milk and another cookie," Tante Sara said. "I'm not much help to you, telling you what you already know. But you're young. You can't find out all these things overnight, but you've got to try. Maybe you should look for another job, something you'd like better. If you liked what you were doing, you wouldn't resent the burden on you so much."

"Maybe," Kate said uncertainly. She had wanted some magic answer from Tante Sara, but she knew with a sigh of despair that there wasn't any such thing. "Maybe I'm the wrong kind of girl to be married to someone like Mike. Maybe he needs a more exciting girl, and I need someone less complicated, someone who wouldn't mind having a simple wife."

"But did you fall in love with such a boy? No. You fell in love with Mike and he with you. Besides, right now, Mike is not complaining about you; you are complaining about yourself," Tante Sara added gently. Then in a sterner voice she said, "You want to be something, but you are afraid to start at the beginning and work at it. Mike cannot live your life for you, Kate. You have to do that for yourself."

"I guess you're right," Kate said meekly. She was exhausted from the evening and from all the talk. "Can I stay here tonight?" she asked. "I'm too tired to take the subway home."

Tante Sara studied her face. "I think it would be better if you went home to your husband," she said. "Take it from an old woman, don't stay angry overnight, don't go to bed on a fight. I'll call up Mike and tell him you are coming home."

Kate smiled at Tante Sara admiringly. "You're quite a person. I wish I had your guts. You never complain, do you? I mean having to give up your home in Germany, going through so much, losing your husband, living alone now. You make me feel like a peanut."

"*Ach*, of course I complain. I complain about the little things. That they don't clean off my sidewalk, that the meat is too fat, that I have too many stairs in my house . . .

I complain all day. About the big things, that is different. Who should I complain to?"

Kate laughed. She gave Tante Sara a hug. "You call Mike and tell him I'm on the way home. He must be worried stiff by now. Good night, dear Tante Sara."

Kate felt better for having talked with Mike's grandmother, and when she came home Mike's face, pale beneath his sunburn, and his anxious eyes filled her with contrition and with love. "I walked all over this neighborhood," Mike said, holding her close. "You scared the wits out of me. Please don't ever do that again, darling. No matter how angry you are at me, no matter what I've done, don't ever walk out that way. I nearly lost my mind."

In Mike's arms, Kate felt comforted. Loving him so much, she surely could find an answer to the muddle they were in.

 FOR A FEW DAYS KATE
tried very hard to forget her problems, to be cheerful and
gay, and devote herself to being Mike's wife. But the re-
sentments were merely pushed back, not resolved. Time
stretched ahead of her in endless days, and the idea of two
more years in her current routine filled her with dread.
She hated the prospect of looking for another job, especially since she had had to pay the employment agency so
much money for getting her the present one.

Later that week Mike brought Jake Bernstein home for
dinner. Kate liked Jake, although she was rather in awe of
him. He was a quiet, thoughtful man, who seemed to have
an amazing store of knowledge on almost every topic
under the sun. Kate had heard him discuss religion, music,

ancient history and archaeology, the contemporary theater, and many novels with equal ease and with the pertinent facts at his fingertips. He also knew simple things such as how long to roast a turkey and the best way to iron a shirt, having demonstrated the latter to Kate one evening by ironing several of Mike's shirts for her.

The minute the two young men walked into the house, Kate sensed that Mike had something up his sleeve. The expression on his face was that of a person with some kind of news, and he followed her around restlessly, peeping into the pots on the stove, asking her how soon dinner would be ready. She wasn't the least bit surprised, when they finally sat down to eat, to hear Mike announce that he and Jake had something they wanted to talk to her about.

"I knew you had something on your mind," Kate said with a smile. "What is it?"

"You told me to find you a job and I have," Mike said. "At least Jake has. He has a great idea for you."

Immediately Kate felt her guard go up. Her job had been the seeming source of so many arguments between herself and Mike that now the mention of it automatically sounded a note of warning. "Oh? What is it?" Kate asked unenthusiastically.

Her tone didn't dampen Mike's zeal. "It's just the thing. Jake, tell her."

"Well, the job itself isn't that marvelous. I don't want to build it up too high. Your husband gets excited easily, as you well know," Jake said with a grin, "but I think you'd like the place and the people. It's with the Settlement House right in the neighborhood, just a few blocks away. You've probably passed it a hundred times—that old brick building over toward the river. They need another paid worker. They don't have much money, and the salary's not great. But you'd be working with a wonderful woman, a good friend of mine, Olga Calgano. She's the only paid worker they have now; the rest are volunteers."

"What would the job be?" Kate asked.

"I think a little bit of everything. The Settlement House is a real community center. The volunteers run several classes for kids and adults. Everyone in the neighborhood adores Olga, and they come to her with all kinds of problems—whether or not to leave their husbands, or how to get rid of their babies' diaper rash. It certainly wouldn't be dull or routine."

"How much does it pay?"

Jake named a figure that was almost ten dollars a week less than Kate was already earning. "We couldn't get along on that," she said spontaneously. "We barely manage as it is. We're not saving a penny."

"We don't have to save now," Mike said. "We're young and there's just the two of us. I think it's important for you to be doing something that you're interested in."

"I don't really care what I'm doing," Kate said, not quite honestly. "As far as I'm concerned my job will only last until you get finished with school. I don't want to work after that. I want to stay home and have a baby. One job's the same as another, and we need money."

Mike looked to Jake for support. "But I don't believe that's true," he said earnestly. "I think what you're doing makes a big difference. It does to me. I don't like seeing you unhappy."

Kate was annoyed and embarrassed. "I think we'd better discuss this when we're alone," she said.

"No, we should discuss it right now. Jake is our friend, he's my oldest friend. We can talk in front of him. He's smart and I respect his judgment."

"Sure, because he agrees with you," Kate said tartly. "I don't like discussing my private business in public."

"A job's not that private," Mike said impatiently. "Jake's gone to the trouble to find this job for you. The least you can do is to be grateful and to discuss it."

"I am grateful. Thank you, Jake. But I don't see what there is to discuss. I can't take less money."

"Maybe after a couple of months it could go up a little," Jake said. "I can't promise that; Olga would know better. Why don't you go and talk to her, Kate, before you make up your mind?"

"Yes, talk to her," Mike urged. "And you know, honey, we can borrow money if we need it. My folks are always asking me if we don't need some money. What if we do go into debt? It's no crime. We'll pay it back when I start working. And my folks wouldn't miss it. They wouldn't be deprived of anything."

"I don't want to borrow," Kate said firmly.

"You're just thinking of yourself." Mike was losing his patience. "You'd rather wreck our marriage than borrow money. You hate that lousy job of yours, and you take it out on me. You're not fooling anybody. You resent having to work while I'm not, and it spills over to everything else, even the meetings I go to. For heaven's sake, Kate, don't be such a stubborn goose."

"I'm not a goose," Kate said indignantly. "What I do resent is your attitude. Not only do you want me to work, but you want to decide what I should work at. You like to mastermind everyone. You're swelled up with your own importance. Well, you're not going to run my life for me. You've been trying to turn me into someone that I'm not ever since I've known you. I don't want to be someone else. If you don't like me the way I am, you shouldn't have married me!" Kate stared at him defiantly.

Mike was clearly hurt and shocked. "That's not fair and it's not true. I'm not trying to push you around. People don't have to stand still; they can change and develop. I think you're terrific and I hate to see you wasting your brain on a dumb job. You have a potential that you're throwing away."

"I guess that's my business if that's what I want to do. I'm happy if you'll leave me alone."

"But you're not happy. That's exactly the point. If you were I wouldn't care. Please, honey, go and see Olga," Mike said pleadingly.

"I'll think about it. The whole discussion is very rude and I'm sure a big bore to Jake."

"Don't mind me," Jake said. "I'll stay out of this, but you've got nothing to lose by going to see Olga. You can see her on Saturday, when you're not working," he suggested.

"I was thinking of going up to Vermont this weekend, to see my mother," Kate said.

Mike was surprised. "You didn't say anything to me about that. Do you want to go alone, or can I come too?"

"I think I'll go alone," Kate said on the spur of the moment. She had been thinking of going to Vermont and had assumed that Mike would go with her. But now, when he asked the question, it suddenly seemed wise to her to go alone. The trip would give her a chance to think things over. She felt confused about herself, her marriage, and the tensions between herself and Mike.

"If that's what you want to do, honey." Mike's eyes were anxious, but he leaned over and kissed her. "It'll probably do you good to get up in the country for a weekend and to see your mother."

No one said anything more about the job, but the subject, Kate knew, was only temporarily tabled.

The air was fresh and clean at the familiar Hebron station. After New York's muggy summer days it was easy to forget what country air smelled like, and Kate breathed it in deeply. She wished she could store it up in her lungs to bring back to the city. But the fresh air gave her a pang of guilt, for having left Mike behind to swelter in their far from cool apartment. Resolutely she told herself her visit had a purpose besides seeing her mother and Judd. It would help both Mike and herself if she could clear her mind and resolve some of their problems. She hadn't asked to be met at the station, and she picked up her small overnight bag for the pleasant walk up to her house.

"Katie, you look so pale and thin!" Mrs. Minton kissed her daughter's cheek. "It's living in New York City. I read in the paper the air is poisoned. Polluted air is what you've been breathing. I don't know why the people there don't do something about it. I wouldn't stand for it." Kate sat down on a kitchen chair and listened to her mother go on about the evils of air pollution. The kitchen was a disorganized mess of vegetables and fruits that her mother was freezing and canning.

"Where's Judd?" Kate interrupted her mother's chatter.

"He had to go mow the minister's lawn, but he'll be back soon. A lot of people don't like Mr. Stuart's sermons, but I think they're beautiful, absolutely beautiful. You'll have to come hear him tomorrow. I suppose you never go to church in New York. It's not the way you were brought up, to run around and forget about church. That's a pretty dress you're wearing. I suppose you paid a lot of money for it in the city. Everything's so expensive there it's hard to believe."

Mrs. Minton went on, not waiting for an answer to any of her questions. Eventually she got around to asking Kate why Mike hadn't come up with her. Kate simply told her that Mike was busy with a lot of homework over the weekend.

"I wouldn't have left my husband alone in New York City over a weekend. I'm not saying that Mike's the kind to run around, but there's always a girl waiting to grab somebody's husband if she has a chance. Men are like children. Leave a baby alone with a box of candy, he'll eat it all up. Same with a man. Leave him in an apartment alone in a big city, he's going to use it. I don't want to worry you, but it's a big mistake. . . ."

In spite of knowing that her mother liked to talk, Kate began to worry. Perhaps she had been a fool to leave Mike in New York. What if Peggy Cannon came over? It was terrible of her not to trust Mike, and yet. . . .

Kate quickly realized that Hebron, Vermont, was about the worst place she could have picked to come to think. When Judd appeared he was more remote than ever, wound up in a life of his own that seemed to consist of cars, motorcycles, and the rock-and-roll music that he played incessantly. Kate was alarmed by the provincial self-absorption of both her mother and Judd. Neither one of them evinced much interest in what her life in New York was like, in her job, or in Mike. Seeing them made her uneasily aware of her own concern with her problems and gave her a desperate urgency to shake herself free of her moody preoccupation with her worries.

Kate's sense of estrangement from her mother and her brother caused her to question her reasons for marrying Mike. Had she been running away from her family? Had she fallen in love with Mike's family as much as with Mike? She remembered how impressed she had been and still was with Mr. and Mrs. Gordon and Tante Sara, with their warmth and their intellectual pursuits, their involvement with the world around them. Mike said that everyone had to be committed to something, and her answer had been that she was committed to him, but maybe that wasn't enough. She certainly didn't want to become like her mother, living in a welter of petty, inconsequential items jumbled together in her head. Kate felt sorry for her mother because she sensed that way back sometime, probably when Mrs. Minton had first decided she wanted to be a teacher, there had been an inquiring mind with a goal and a direction.

Kate did not go to church on Sunday morning because, again on the spur of the moment, she decided she wanted to stop in Boston on her way home, to see Candy. There was a bus coming through a little after nine that she could take, and she caught it.

Being on the move seemed to soothe her restlessness, and Kate enjoyed sitting in the bus and watching the little villages and towns go by. She felt somewhat as if she were on an adventure or a quest, although she wasn't at all sure what she was seeking.

Returning to the old dorm was in a way more like coming home than home itself. The downstairs reception room, as always, held the remains of last night's party in the sagging imprint on its overstuffed sofas, the fingerprints on the tinny upright piano, the empty bags of potato chips, and the few lone pretzels in their large bowls. The smell of floor varnish, perfume, and food saturated the halls. Kate felt a strong nostalgia for it all as she ran lightly up the steps to Candy's room. It was not the same one that the two girls had shared—with Kate gone, Candy had preferred a single—but it was filled with familiar furnishings that Kate knew well, including several articles she had left behind.

"The room looks marvelous," Kate said admiringly, hugging Candy warmly. "And so do you. I'm so glad to see you."

"Let me look at you." Candy stood off to study her friend's face. "You look different."

"Different how?"

"I don't know. Maybe married different. You look okay, skinnier, and . . . I don't know, just different."

"You make me feel old."

"How are things going?" Candy asked.

"Not so hot. Goodness, I didn't want to start talking about myself right away!"

"Why not? You came here to talk, didn't you?"

Kate gave Candy a grateful look. "It's polite to ask about you first," she said with a grin.

"I can tell you about me in two minutes. Nothing. Absolutely nothing. I'm not seeing Tommy anymore; it was getting too complicated. And now my life is as dull as an old television show. I'm dying to fall in love, but there's no one around. Everyone's either going with someone or is a dog. That's the story of my life, dearie. Hope yours is more exciting, at least."

"I don't know that it is," Kate said.

"How's Mike?" Candy asked.

"Mike's fine. I think he loves law school, and he's all excited about electing someone to Congress. I think he's having a good time."

"And you? You sound like you're not in it," Candy said shrewdly.

"That's one of the troubles. I'm not." Talking to Candy was marvelous, Kate thought. They understood each other so well that they could pick up an intimate conversation as if they'd seen each other the day before.

"So come on, give. Tell me what's going on." Candy made herself comfortable on the bed and motioned to Kate to sit down. "Stop pacing around the room."

Kate settled down in Candy's one armchair and quickly described her dull job, her fear that she was proving to be the wrong girl for Mike, the petty arguments they got into. She even told her about Peggy Cannon.

"Are you seriously worried about that girl?" Candy asked.

"I suppose not. I feel she's kind of a warning to me, though. I worry so that one of these days I'll lose Mike—if not to her, to someone like her."

"But what are you doing about it?" Candy demanded.

"What can I do? I'm me, and Mike's Mike. Neither of us is going to change. I suppose one of the troubles is that I didn't know Mike very well when we got married. But I can't talk to him the way I can to you."

Candy laughed. "Of course not."

"It's not funny." Kate was disconsolate.

"I know it's not funny. But honey, of course you can't talk to Mike the way you talk to a girl friend. Boys are different. Don't you see, too much talk knocks the sex right out of it. If a boy is a pal, like a girl friend, you're not going to want to make love and kiss him and all that jazz. You and Mike are in love with each other, so you *can't* talk all the time. It would get too sticky. You're too sensitive to each other."

"I always thought you should be able to talk to your husband about everything," Kate said wistfully.

"That's a lot of rot. Most married couples don't talk about anything except what they're going to eat for dinner, or if the rent got paid. But that's awful too. Sure you should be able to talk to Mike, but I think you're expecting too much. You said that neither you or Mike will change. Well, you're going to have to."

"Why me?" Kate threw her head back.

"Because you're the wife, that's why. Don't ask me how I know all this, but I do. You go around with blinkers on, living in some romantic world, the old dancing in the dark bit. If you want to stay married to Mike, you'll have to do some changing."

"You sound like a magazine article," Kate remarked.

"I do not. They tell you it's all light and roses. I say you have to work at this. If you think of yourself as a drudge, you're sure as anything going to be one. So get off that track right now. The trouble with you is you love Mike, but you don't really care about what he does. It's a pretty picayune love, if you ask me."

"How can you say that!" Kate was shocked and hurt.

"Because it's true," Candy said more gently. "You want Mike all to yourself, but you'll never have him that way. He's too interesting to devote himself entirely to being your husband. Kate, you've got what it takes to make yourself a great person in your own right."

Kate grimaced. "I'm so tired of people telling me I don't live up to my potential. That's all I heard in school, and then in college. It's boring. I am what I am."

"Sometimes I want to shake you. You have some emotional block or something, or you're stubborn. Maybe it's because you're so pretty—you ride along on that. Or you're just plain lazy. I don't know."

"What does everyone want me to be? I wish someone would tell me!"

"Anything but a drifter. Being a pretty girl isn't enough.

You've got a brain, but you refuse to use it." Candy's voice was rising dangerously high.

"Don't scream at me," Kate said crossly

"I'm sorry, but you make me mad."

"I can't turn myself into something that I'm not. I really can't get excited about electing some Irishman to Congress. How do I know he's any better than anyone else? Politics bore me."

"Then find something that you *can* get excited about."

Kate sighed. "I was excited about getting married. I thought that would be enough to last me for a long time."

"Maybe I'm talking a lot of nonsense," Candy said kindly. "I'm no oracle with all the answers." The expression on Candy's face was sympathetic, but Kate was sure her friend still believed that what she had said was right.

Although Kate gained some comfort from talking with Candy, her sense of isolation was no less sharp than before. Candy's bounce took her on to talk about many things—her courses, the girls in the dorm, all the things Kate felt she had left behind. She didn't really want to be back at college; that was not what made her sad. It was the fear of having left something known for something unknown and unsure.

When Kate left Candy to go back to New York, she felt as alone as she ever had before, and that aloneness was not wiped out, as she felt it should be, by her eager anticipation to get home to Mike.

9

THE FOLLOWING SATUR-
day morning Kate made up her mind to go to the Settlement House to see Jake's friend Olga Calgano. But she
didn't want Mike to know. The week had been a strange
one. Neither she nor Mike had brought up the subject of
her job, and while there had been no intimate conversation
between them, they had both been trying their best to be
understanding. Kate didn't say a word when Mike went
out two evenings campaigning, and he made a point of
getting home early, before she had gone to bed. One night
he surprised her by having dinner all ready when she came
home. The meal was pretty much bought pre-prepared, but
Kate was touched by his doing it.

"I have so much to learn about living with a man," she

wrote to Candy, when she thanked her for the visit. Kate wondered if she, herself, could ever understand some things, which she could not talk about. For instance, could she ever understand the separateness between her and Mike, when in the beautiful and searing passion of their lovemaking they were so much as one? How, in the sweet darkness of the night, could they embrace and express their love so deeply, and then in the cold dawn of day go rushing off in different directions as if they were strangers?

Candy had accused her of wanting Mike all to herself. Was that wrong when you were still a bride? She *did* want Mike to herself. She wanted to be with him every minute of her waking day as well as beside him in bed at night. But between his school, his homework, and the election campaign, her job, her housework, and the marketing, they only had dinner together many evenings and met in the dark in bed. Why couldn't life stop and give them a chance to catch up?

This morning Kate intended to make her own decision about the job at the Settlement House. She would tell Mike if it was offered to her, and whether or not she took it, after the interview.

The day was rainy. Mike, who was studying with his

heavy law books spread out over the dining table, was surprised to see Kate dressed to go out.

"I have to do some marketing," Kate explained.

"If you wait till this afternoon I'll go with you," Mike offered.

"I'll do it now, and we can do something else this afternoon," Kate said.

"You sure you're going marketing?" Kate usually wore old clothes around the house on Saturday, but now she had on her best cotton "working" dress and a rain cape.

"I really have a date," she said teasingly.

"I'll kill him," Mike said, and gave her a kiss.

The Settlement House was surrounded by ancient tenements, in an even shabbier neighborhood than theirs. The street was crowded with open stalls of unappetizing food and cheap merchandise. Kate was learning to have an affection not for the poverty, but for the mixed groups living so closely together. They seemed to spend their lives on the street, eating, playing, nursing their babies, making love. Though they were mysterious and foreign to the girl from Vermont, they were warm and alive, and she could see both humor and tragedy imprinted on their faces.

Mrs. Calgano had a desk in a small room inside the

brick building, and when Kate introduced herself she was greeted cordially. "Jake told me about you, and I've been hoping you would come over to see me," Mrs. Calgano said. She was a tall, statuesque woman, her black hair streaked with gray, and her fine, dark eyes deeply set in a round, cheerful face. She gave an impression of great calm strength, and Kate liked her immediately. She could see why the people in the neighborhood would easily turn to her for help and advice.

Mrs. Calgano explained the job and the workings of the Settlement House to Kate. They ran many classes, both for children and adults, "everything from English to finger painting," as Mrs. Calgano put it. They had a kiln for pottery work, and they depended on volunteers to teach. "People come in here for everything—advice on how to feed their babies, how to get a divorce, how to keep their kids in school. The other day a Jewish grandmother came to me in tears because her married daughter won't keep a kosher house and she can't go there to eat anymore. We try to help them as much as we can. We have many referrals, and we keep records, so there's a lot of paper work to do. We refer people to clinics, to psychiatrists, to special schools, to rabbis and ministers and priests, to lawyers, and to many social and welfare agencies. I guess we're kind of a clearing house for all the problems in the vicinity. Outside of our classes, the most we can do is send people to the right place for help and try to see that they get it."

"It sounds wonderful," Kate said enthusiastically.

Mrs. Calgano went into more detail about the job of her assistant that Kate would have. She would handle a lot of paper work, register pupils for the classes, keep track of the volunteers. "They're a pretty reliable bunch, but often someone gets sick at the last minute and we have to dig up a replacement. You'll meet all kinds of people here," Mrs. Calgano said.

While they had been talking a young Puerto Rican boy, who looked to be in his early teens, had been hovering around the door, peering in anxiously at Mrs. Calgano. "What is it, Jimmy? You can come in," she called.

As the boy entered, Mrs. Calgano said, "This is Mrs. Gordon, who may be coming here to work. And this is Jimmy Juarez, who is one of the best helpers I have. He cleans up, he gets me coffee, he's a great help." Jimmy looked at her with admiring eyes, although he was greatly agitated, and pushed a piece of paper in front of her. "It came this morning," he said excitedly. "A man brought it."

Mrs. Calgano glanced at the paper and showed it to Kate. "An eviction notice. I've been expecting this. We got a stay for them a couple of times, but I'm afraid we won't be able to again. I'll come and see your mother," she said to Jimmy. "Tell her I'll be over this afternoon."

When the boy had left Mrs. Calgano sighed. "I suppose they'll have to move in with relatives, into some crowded place that already has too many people in it."

"Can't they find another apartment?" Kate asked.

"It's not that easy. They've been living behind a store. An awful place by our standards, but Mrs. Juarez fixed it up very nicely. Now the store's been sold, and the people who bought it want to move in. It costs money to move, and the Juarezes haven't found any place they can afford. There are five children; one of them's retarded and needs a lot of care. I'd hate to see that family have to move into one room."

Kate was shocked. "One room for seven people! That's awful."

"I'm afraid you're going to see and hear worse than that around here. We do the best we can."

Kate decided she would take the job. Mrs. Calgano mentioned the same salary that Jake had. Little as it was, it sounded like a lot in the bare surroundings and after hearing the Juarez story. She pushed from her mind the worry of how she and Mike would manage.

When she came outside the rain had stopped, and Kate hurried home to tell her news to Mike, completely forgetting to stop for her shopping.

"It's great, just great!" Mike was delighted. "Let's celebrate this afternoon."

Kate was bubbling with excitement. She told Mike the story about the Juarez family. "You should have seen that boy. He was beautiful. You'll make a do-gooder of me yet."

"Don't use that word. I hate it. *Do-gooder* implies something I don't like."

Kate looked at him in surprise. "I thought that's what you wanted."

"Are you taking this job because I want you to or because you want to?"

Kate shrugged. "A little bit of both, I guess." Still unsure of her feelings, she didn't want to get into a serious conversation with Mike about her motives now.

The day turned into a sunny one that was not too hot, and Mike and Kate wandered around the Village looking at the outdoor art exhibit and the shop windows. The day was a glorious one for Kate. She felt closer to Mike than she had in weeks, and she also had an awareness of herself that she had all but lost. She enjoyed the admiring glances that came her way from the men they passed on the street and was amused by the tightening, possessive grip Mike took on her arm at the same time. The thought occurred to her sometime that day that scrubbing floors and making ends meet was not the part of her that Mike wanted to see. Mike's image of her was that of a beautiful, talented, and interesting girl—and if she could reflect that image she might sometime even find those qualities within herself.

They brought home a bottle of wine and invited Gary and Mia to have supper with them. The Mitchells were enthusiastic about Kate's new job. "You'll save carfare," practical Mia said.

Kate admitted that she could hardly wait for her two weeks' notice to run out, so that she could start working.

At her desk in Mrs. Calgano's office, Kate turned to her day's calendar. She couldn't believe it was Friday, her first week at the Settlement House had passed so quickly. This morning she had to call up the Legal Aid Society to see if Mrs. Lopez had kept her appointment the day before.

Mrs. Lopez had been deserted by her husband and was trying to get support for her four children; Mrs. Calgano had made several appointments for her with the Legal Aid Society, but Mrs. Lopez never kept them. The answer was the same today: she hadn't shown up. Poor people, Kate was discovering, were suspicious of help. They didn't want to get mixed up with institutions and organizations; they were shy and timid about seeking outside aid. She wished they had some of Mike's spirit, but most of the people she had seen in the past few days seemed to accept their unhappy lot with a weary resignation.

The progress they made was discouraging. There was so much tragedy and poverty, and the problems seemed endless. This week Kate had seen men with large families out of work, children who had no shoes to wear to school, sick old people without any place to live, families fighting and breaking up. A great deal of Kate's work consisted of referring people to other agencies, and when she made the telephone calls or wrote the letters that Mrs. Calgano dictated, she felt she was reaching out into a tremendous void. On the phone she often had to speak to three or four different persons before she got the right one; the red tape appeared interminable.

"It all takes so long," she complained to Mrs. Calgano.

"Mrs. Schloss needs a nursing home now, not next week."

"I know, I know." Mrs. Calgano was sympathetic with Kate's impatience. "We can only do what we can."

Someone was coming through the door, and Kate looked up. It was Mrs. Juarez, mother of Jimmy, the boy Kate had met the day of her interview. She had been coming in to see Mrs. Calgano every few days, because of her worry about being evicted, and today she had brought nine-year-old Carmen, the child who was retarded, with her.

While the women talked, Carmen stood silently by Kate's desk, her big eyes watching Kate type. The child's sallow, thin face was so sad-looking Kate wished she could think of something to make her smile. Her attempts at conversation went unanswered. On an impulse she went to the small shelf of children's books they had and brought out a picture book. Showing Carmen the pictures, Kate started reading her the story. It was hard to tell whether the little girl understood the words, but her eyes were glued to the pictures avidly.

"She don't understand nothing," Mrs. Juarez said protestingly, when she saw what was going on, as if she wanted to protect Carmen from being exposed or hurt.

"But she does," Kate declared. "I think she does understand."

Then Kate had an inspiration. She gave Carmen a piece of paper and a red pencil, and drew a figure first to get her started.

Carmen took the pencil and made scribbles with it. They weren't really pictures, but the child was delighted and she finally gave Kate a shy smile.

"Look, Carmen," Kate said, "this is how you draw a cat."

Now Mrs. Juarez determinedly took away the pencil and paper from her child. "She don't understand," she repeated brusquely. "We leave her alone." She drew Carmen to her, but Carmen let out a loud howl at losing her paper and pencil. Mrs. Calgano and Kate persuaded Mrs. Juarez to let the child keep them.

When they left, Kate told Mrs. Calgano, "I'm sure Carmen did understand something. I'm sure of it."

Walking home that night Kate thought about Carmen Juarez. She couldn't get the child out of her mind; she sensed there was something imprisoned behind those big, sad, brown eyes. Yet Kate felt hesitant and shy about telling Mike what had happened that day. Would he think she was foolish and sentimental, to be so concerned about one nine-year-old retarded child? He wanted to do such big things—tackle all of poverty and segregation, get at the root of things and change the world. She could never explain to him how much satisfaction she had received from today's small success with Carmen.

10

KATE COULD HEAR THE volunteer workers chatting in the small lounge adjacent to her office. Though she had been in her new job several weeks, the young women who came to help still made her a little uncomfortable. She thought of them as "the uptown girls," with their chic suits, high heels, and beauty-parlor hairdos. Mrs. Calgano said they had all been fashionable debutantes. "We are very grateful for what they do for us," she had added firmly.

The volunteers were getting ready for the exhibit of artwork and pottery that was to open that evening. "You must come tonight," Mrs. Calgano said to Kate, "and bring your husband. I think he will find it interesting."

"We'll be here," Kate said confidently.

There were coffee and doughnuts for that evening to take care of, letters to type for Mrs. Calgano. . . . Kate was typing away when a tiny, shrivelled-up Negro man came in with a picture in his hand.

"I heard you were having an art show here," he said. "Can I put this in?" He handed Kate a crayon picture of a farm. It was done with great care for detail, and Kate was sure the little man had spent a lot of time on it. The art exhibit was really for the work done in the classes in the Settlement House, but Kate quickly decided she couldn't refuse him.

"Certainly. I'll give it to the girls to hang up. Will you come back tonight to see the show?"

The man nodded his head. He put his picture on Kate's desk, smoothing the paper lovingly. "Take good care of this, miss, please."

"Don't worry. And when the show is over you can have it back," Kate told him.

This job, Kate thought to herself, couldn't be more different from life with the Gabriel brothers! Instead of working with numbers and figures on sheets of paper, she was dealing with real people, many of whom she saw face to face. The knowledge that what she was doing was affecting their lives gave her a sense of elation.

The way Mrs. Calgano helped the people who came to the Settlement House constantly impressed Kate and made her aware of how much the older woman knew, both as a psychologist and a social worker. She was pleased and flattered that Mrs. Calgano took her into her confidence, discussing the many problems that came across her desk. In turn, Kate found herself talking to her new friend about some of her own problems.

And to Kate's delight, Mrs. Juarez had been bringing Carmen to the Settlement House often. At first she had been a little shamefaced. "She pulled me over here," she said, gesturing toward Carmen. "She wanna come here." But Kate was delighted. She sat and showed Carmen pictures, or let her "draw" some more. They didn't come every day—"I'm too busy for this," Mrs. Juarez said, still pretending she didn't think much of it—but each time Kate worked patiently with the child, feeling a warm empathy between them. She was positive Carmen was getting something out of their sessions. She certainly enjoyed them and wanted to come back.

The visits were giving Mrs. Calgano and Kate an opportunity to point out to Mrs. Juarez that with proper teaching and attention, Carmen could be developed beyond her present level, even if she was retarded. Last week Mrs.

Juarez had finally agreed grudgingly to go so far as to let Mrs. Calgano try to place Carmen in a special school. The step was in the right direction.

That evening, when Kate reminded Mike that they had to go over to the art exhibit, his face clouded over. "But I can't, sweetheart. We're having a terribly important meeting over at O'Donnell's headquarters. We're getting a mailing out and we've got to discuss what we want to say. I have to be there."

"But this is important, too; it's the opening of the exhibit. It wouldn't hurt Mr. O'Donnell to drop in, either."

"I'm sure he'd love to if he could, but no one told him about it. Anyway, this meeting was just called because the opposition has been saying some nasty things about him we want to squelch. Jake asked me to write a statement."

Kate's face showed her disappointment. "Please, darling, don't be angry." Mike looked at her pleadingly. "Once this campaign is over we can do lots of things together."

"If we *are* together," Kate murmured.

Mike gave her a swift look. "Don't say that. What do you want me to do? You want me to pull out of the campaign now?"

Kate looked at him with troubled eyes. "I thought if I

changed my job things would be different. But you don't care about what I do, do you? Why did you want to get married, Mike?"

"Because I love you. What better reason? But maybe you should have married someone who would come home and watch television with you every night."

"Maybe I should have. It might be nice some nights." There was a deep frown between her eyes. "It's not so much what you do, Mike, it's your attitude toward me. I feel as if I'm some kind of appendage, who should be around when you want me and disappear when you don't. I can't live that way. I can't put on an invisible cloak when you ring the bell."

"That's not fair, and it's not true. It might be more correct to say that you don't care about what I do. You've hated this election campaign from the beginning." Mike was pacing back and forth as he did when he was angry or upset, his face white and tense.

"Yes, I do hate it. Meetings and politics bore me. I'm not a crusader. I like to enjoy life, to have a good time, not change the world."

"Yes, you'd like to live with your head in the sand. What did Candy used to say? That you were dancing in the dark. How can you go to that Settlement House every day and not see what's going on around you?" Mike demanded.

"It's to the Settlement House that I wanted *you* to go tonight," Kate said tartly. "I care about people, but you don't. You're just puffed up with your own importance, getting out statements and writing releases, but the people involved don't matter."

Mike stopped his pacing and stood in front of Kate. "What do you want me to do? Once you said you loved me because I am what I am, because I am involved and I want to change things. Now you hate me for the same reasons."

"I don't hate you," Kate said quickly. "I love you, that's the trouble. If I hated you I wouldn't care, and I could walk out that door easily. But I feel trapped. I guess living with a person and loving a person are two different things."

"Can't you go to this art exhibit alone? You won't be by yourself. You'll know everyone who's there. Why should I have to go when I have something else to do?" Mike appeared sincerely perplexed.

"Oh, I suppose I can go alone, but I shouldn't have to. Not when I have a husband. The girls around the Settlement who don't have boy friends come in alone, and I feel sorry for them. I don't want to be one of them, going places by myself at night."

"You're a big girl. And you won't be out late." Mike was looking at her now with an amused smile.

"You don't understand," Kate said impatiently. "I feel as if I'm half of everything. Half a wife and half a paycheck and half a housekeeper. I'm only half educated. I couldn't go on and do anything professionally now even if I wanted to, because I didn't finish college!" Kate blurted out the last defiantly.

"So that's it. Now you resent not having finished college and you're blaming me. If you really wanted to, you could take some courses at night."

"Oh yes, after working all day and marketing and cooking and cleaning. Sure, I could take courses at night. That's a really brilliant idea." Kate was close to tears.

"What do you want me to do, darling? You tell me, just tell me, what you want me to do." Mike's voice was gentle.

"I don't know. I think the whole thing stinks. I suppose I should shut up and be cheerful and brave and glad that you're in law school and doing things you enjoy, and I should be patient and not complain, but I feel as if I'm getting a raw deal."

"The trouble with you is you want a modern husband, but an old-fashioned marriage. You want to be pampered and spoiled and waited on by an adoring male, but the only male who would do that is a goof you couldn't stand for a minute. Stop reading the ladies' magazines and grow up!" Mike pulled a comb out of his pocket and went over to the mirror and combed his hair. "I've got to go now. All this talk isn't going to get us anywhere anyhow. Go to your exhibit, honey, and I'll get home as fast as I can."

He leaned over and kissed her.

When the door closed behind Mike, Kate sat down and burst into tears. They were tears of exhaustion, frustration, and bewilderment. Mike had said one thing that struck home. She *did* want a husband to pamper her and adore her. But didn't every woman want that? And what was wrong with it? She wanted to indulge her femininity, not be another's pillar of strength.

Wearily Kate washed the supper dishes and went to bed. She didn't feel like seeing strong Mrs. Calgano, or the chic volunteers, or even sturdy, cheerful Mrs. Juarez. She wanted to be alone with her longing and her helplessness.

The next morning Kate was up early. She finished

breakfast and was trying to balance their joint checking account when Mike came out of the bedroom sleepily. "Good morning, darling. How was the art exhibit?"

"Good morning . . . coffee's on the stove. I didn't go last night."

"Oh?"

"I didn't feel like it," Kate said, avoiding his eyes. "Mike, I don't think we're going to have the rent money this month."

"How come?" Mike poured himself a cup of coffee and sat down opposite Kate.

"I guess because I'm earning less. I can stretch it so far and no farther."

"I'm not blaming you, honey. Well, I'll borrow some money from my folks."

Kate looked up and met his gaze. "What ever happened to the part-time job you were going to get?"

"You know what happened. O'Donnell's campaign. I thought that was more important."

"More important than paying the rent?" Kate's wide eyes were searching his face.

"In a way, yes. It's only a few weeks until November, then it'll be all over. I'll get a job then. In the meantime, the rent will get paid. Don't worry about it."

"Everything always has to be done your way doesn't it, Mike?"

"I have to live according to my values," Mike said soberly.

Kate stood up. "I'm going over to work early this morning. There'll be a lot of people coming in to see the exhibit."

Mike looked at her with a troubled face. "You've been carrying a heavy burden, honey. Don't think I'm unaware of it. But let me help in my way. I'll get the money for the rent. Borrowing is no sin."

"I guess there isn't much choice now."

Walking over to the Settlement House Kate wondered if she hadn't exchanged one set of problems for another by changing her job. She was certainly more involved with her work now and vitally interested in it, but instead of its drawing her closer to Mike it seemed to be taking her farther away. She was pulled in one direction, he another.

"Of course you react differently," Mrs. Calgano said, when Kate explained why she hadn't shown up the previous evening. "Not only are you different people, but there's such a thing as male and female reactions. You react more emotionally to people, Mike more objectively to conditions. We need both in this world. Give up the notion of wanting to be the same. I do wish you had a college degree, though."

"Why?"

"I could get a fine job for you. Especially if you went on and took a Master's in psychology or social work. What are you going to do about yourself, Kate? Why don't you finish up and get your degree?"

"How can I now? I have to work."

"You could still take some courses. I think I could arrange for you to work here and go to school."

"I'm afraid I'm not that ambitious. I'm having a hard enough time as it is, without taking on more."

"It's not always how much you do," Mrs. Calgano said gently. "It's your reason for doing it."

"I know. *Motivation* is a very popular word these days. My adviser at college used it all the time."

When Kate returned from lunch that afternoon Mrs. Calgano called out to her excitedly. "Good news, Kate. I've found a place for Carmen Juarez!" Mrs. Calgano named a well-known school for retarded and disturbed children.

"How wonderful!" Kate was so excited she wanted to kiss Mrs. Calgano. "Will you tell Mrs. Juarez tonight?"

Mrs. Calgano's eyes twinkled. "Why don't you go by this afternoon and tell her? You've taken over Carmen completely anyway."

Kate flushed with pride. She had been hoping Mrs. Calgano would let her call on the Juarezes, but she wouldn't have dared suggest it. "I hope Mrs. Juarez will really let her go," she said thoughtfully.

"I think she will, thanks to you. You've done a wonderful job with that little girl, and it's made her mother see what is possible."

Kate felt as if she had been handed a million dollars. A small success like this one was worth all the heartache and discouragement and waiting. If a single person in this jungle of misery could be helped, she thought, everything else became worthwhile.

"You know, the Juarezes still haven't found a place to live, and their time is almost up in that apartment," Mrs. Calgano went on. She had her elbows on her desk, her face resting between her two hands. "Would you tell Mrs. Juarez I may have a lead on a place for her?"

"Sure." Kate tackled the rest of her day's work with a renewed energy and hope.

She left the Settlement House a little early and on her way to the Juarezes' picked up a coloring book for little

Carmen. Kate was both excited with her news for the family and apprehensive about how it would be received. The problem had been not only to find a proper place for the child, but to persuade Mrs. Juarez to let her "baby" go.

Mrs. Juarez was in the midst of cooking when Kate arrived. Despite the fact that she had been mentally prepared, Kate was appalled by the condition of the family's home. Why were they so upset about giving up such a place? The tiny apartment in the back of the grocery store had a primitive oil stove, plaster that was crumbling off the ceiling, and holes in the floor.

The kitchen, however, was filled with the smells of rich cheese and meats and pastry baking. "I'm getting ready for a party," Mrs. Juarez announced. "Tomorrow is Jimmy's birthday and our wedding anniversary. Will you come tomorrow night, and bring your husband?"

"I'd love to, if we can," Kate told her.

"Please, please, you must come. You never been to a Puerto Rican party. We have nice music, lots to eat, we all have a good time. You come with your husband."

"Yes, we'll come," Kate promised. She loved Mrs. Juarez for her cheerfulness, her ability to switch to gaiety from a preoccupation with her troubles. Kate gave her Mrs.

Calgano's message about the possibility of a place to live.

"She's a wonderful woman," Mrs. Juarez remarked. "Maybe she find us someplace to move. Here, taste these cookies, see how you like them."

"They're delicious," Kate said, biting into the warm, sweet cake.

She had given Carmen the coloring book, and the child was busily crayoning in it. Kate was trying to think of the best way to present the fact that a school had been found for Carmen. "I have more good news for you. Mrs. Calgano has found a wonderful place for Carmen. It's one of the best schools in the East," she added hurriedly, watching Mrs. Juarez's face close over. "They can do marvelous things for her. They'll have room for her in a few weeks."

"She too young to go away. She better off at home."

"You can visit her often. It wouldn't be forever. Maybe she'll stay there a year or so . . . they can help her so much." Kate's voice was pleading.

Mrs. Juarez sighed heavily. "We'll see. We think about it." But she put out her hand and patted Kate's arm. "You a good girl. You and Mrs. Calgano, you good people. Very kind. We'll see."

"You have to give her a chance, Mrs. Juarez," Kate said

earnestly. "They have wonderful doctors at this school, and I know they can help her."

As she left the warm atmosphere of Mrs. Juarez's home, Kate realized why this place meant so much to the family. Their futile attempts to cover up the dinginess with paint and religious pictures told her the answer. It was theirs, and theirs only; they did not have to share it with another family.

11

"I'M NOT GIVING YOU much to eat tonight," Kate told Mike. "There'll be lots of food at the Juarezes'."

The phone rang while they were eating, and Mike got up to answer it. Kate could hear his voice plainly. "I can't. It's out of the question. I'm going someplace with Kate. I simply can't do it." After a few seconds, he said, "It's impossible." Another pause, and then, "All right, I'll stop over for half an hour, but that's it. I'm telling you right now, not a minute longer." He put the phone down with a bang.

"What's up?"

"Another crisis over at headquarters." He looked at Kate beseechingly. "Please don't blow your top. You go over to the Juarezes', and I'll be there in half an hour. I swear it."

"You look scared. Are you scared of me?" Kate asked in surprise.

"You bet I am. I'm getting to be like all the rest of the American husbands, scared stiff of my wife."

"Woof, woof, I'm ferocious," Kate said with a forced laugh, but her eyes were troubled.

After supper they left the house together. "I'll be there before you know it."

"I hope so," Kate said.

When Kate arrived at the Juarezes' she found their tiny place packed with friends and relatives, but the atmosphere was more like that of a wake than a party. Instead of the music and gaiety she had expected, Mrs. Juarez was in tears. "They want to throw my furniture out on the street," she sobbed. "All my things, on the street." Kate was shocked. From the babble of voices as everyone tried to explain to her at once, she found out that the Juarez family was finally being evicted. They had to be out by midnight, and Mr. Juarez was off trying to find a truck for their meagre but precious possessions.

"I don't know where we will go," Jimmy said to her sadly. "At my cousin's house the children have measles, at my aunt's they already live in two rooms, seven of them—"

"You can't stay on the street!" Kate was outraged. "And all this beautiful food your mother made for the party!" Kate couldn't believe that such a thing could happen in a great city like New York. "There must be something we can do."

Jimmy shrugged his shoulders. "Nothing we can do anymore."

Kate looked at the small Juarez children playing in a corner, little Carmen hugging an empty milk carton to her breast. The untouched plates of pastries and food were laid out on a table.

"You come and stay in our apartment," Kate said impetuously. "There's plenty of room there for you. Mike and I can live with his grandmother in Brooklyn until you find a place."

Jimmy looked at her unbelievingly. "You mean you will give us your apartment?"

"I'll lend it to you, until you find a place to stay. You can all move in there and Mike and I will move out. It's just temporary," she cautioned Jimmy.

He ran to his mother with excited eyes. "Mrs. Gordon is giving us her apartment," he cried. "We can stay there until we find a place!" Kate was embarrassed by the tears and the hugs. Every guest at the party, most of whom she didn't know, came and shook her hand or kissed her.

"Now we have the party," Mrs. Juarez cried. "Come, everybody eat."

Mrs. Calgano had just arrived. "Where is your husband?" she asked Kate.

"He should be along any minute," Kate said.

When Mrs. Calgano heard the news, she took Kate's hand in hers. "That is a splendid and generous thing to do," she said. "Is it going to be all right with Mike? Perhaps you should have asked him first."

"I'm sure Mike will agree." There was no question in Kate's mind. "He always wants to be doing things."

"But to give up your own apartment is a little different. If he had done it without consulting you, mightn't you have been a little irked?"

"It's only temporary," she murmured, but she looked at Mrs. Calgano thoughtfully. "I never thought of that. I guess I wouldn't have liked it if Mike had done it." Kate realized that she would have been furious if Mike had offered their apartment to a strange family without even discussing it with her. "But what can I do? It's too late now." She looked at the older woman helplessly.

"There's nothing you can do. I think Mike will understand. But remember this evening, Kate. See how easy it is to get caught up with something when you are involved? Two people can't always act as one. Sometimes one has to count on the other going along with him."

The words hit home. But where *was* Mike? He had promised to be there at least an hour ago.

It was after ten when Mr. Juarez arrived with an old pick-up truck he had borrowed. And still no Mike. By this time the party was in full swing. Jimmy was playing his guitar, the food was being eaten, and everyone was talking and laughing gaily, except the little children who had fallen asleep rolled up together on the bed. The men made a game of loading up the truck, with Mrs. Juarez directing them. She spoke so quickly in Spanish Kate couldn't understand a word. Back and forth she ran protecting her things with a blanket, then a shawl, as if she were moving a houseful of precious antiques.

Mrs. Calgano left. Miserable because Mike had never arrived, Kate asked Jimmy to walk her home. She wanted to make the apartment ready for the Juarezes to move in. A superintendent and his wife lived in the basement, and Kate thought there might be room down there to store temporarily the Juarezes' things.

"It is very nice of you, very nice," Jimmy kept repeating.

"Forget it," Kate told him. She was feeling anxious about Mike—he had promised so faithfully to come to the party that she wondered if something had happened to him—and she was also apprehensive about what he would say when she told him the Juarez family was moving into their apartment.

Jimmy pulled her back from the curb as a police car came screaming around the corner. "I wonder what's up," he said.

In the next block they saw a crowd gathered. A fight seemed to be going on. One of Paul O'Donnell's sound trucks was there, and someone—probably Mr. O'Donnell —was trying to talk above the noise of the crowd, attempting to get order. But men were scuffling with each other, and eggs and tomatoes had obviously been thrown. Kate saw a couple of rough-looking young men hurtling themselves against the outer fringe of the crowd, shouting, "Throw O'Donnell out. Send the Commie back where he belongs!"

Kate was furious. "He's no Commie," she told Jimmy heatedly. "I know he isn't. And he belongs right here. He was born right in this neighborhood."

Jimmy was unperturbed. "They always fight down here. Those fellows don't know right from wrong; they just want to fight."

"I bet that's where my husband is," Kate cried in distress. "I bet he's in that crowd with Mr. O'Donnell." She started running toward the crowd, with Jimmy following her. "Be careful," Jimmy screamed after her. "Be careful! They're rough."

But there was no stopping Kate. She was positive she would find Mike there. He would be the first to stand up against roughnecks like those hecklers.

And there he was—exchanging blows with another man. "Mike!" Kate screamed. Then things happened very quickly. The policemen were out of the police car, trying to break up the fighting, and Kate, with a cry of anguish, saw Mike sink down under a blow from a policeman's nightstick.

"Leave him alone, leave him alone!" Kate sobbed, beating her fists against the chest of the policeman. "How dare you hit him!"

"He was fighting, miss." The policeman held Kate's wrists tightly in his hands. She struggled loose and started beating her hands against him again. "Leave him alone!" Mike staggered to his feet, only to fall down again. Before

Kate knew what was happening a couple of other policemen carried Mike, who was bleeding, over to a police car,
and she and a group of others were herded into a paddy
wagon. She had completely lost Jimmy.

"But I didn't do anything," Kate moaned. "They hit my
husband. . . ."

Inside the paddy wagon Kate was terrified. With the
exception of an elderly Negro woman and an outraged
Italian woman who was screaming epithets in Italian, the
others with her were all men. When the policeman closed
and locked the back door and stood facing them with a
stony face, she thought she was going to suffocate. Kate
had seen these sinister small, black trucks go screaming
through the city, but not in her wildest fears had she ever
imagined she would land in one. She tried desperately to
keep herself from panicking. The smell in the wagon—a
sickening combination of stale tobacco, vomit, and un-
clean bodies—was nauseating. The faces surrounding her
were varied, but all sullen and unfriendly. She wondered
if any of the "good guys" were in here with her, or if these
men were all hecklers. If any of O'Donnell's people were
here she didn't recognize them.

And what was happening to Mike? He had looked
awful as he was carried away into the police car, his face

covered with blood. Was he being taken to a police station, or to a hospital? Kate's anger and frustration by no means helped to calm her. The irony that she, of all people—who had done nothing except try to protect her husband—should be carted away upset her as much as anything. She had always thought she was obviously an innocent, not a troublemaker.

At the police station they were all herded into a big room lighted by a bright, naked bulb and lined up before a rather handsome young sergeant seated at a huge desk. He ordered them to come forward and be fingerprinted.

Kate was indignant. "I'm not a criminal! Why should I be fingerprinted?"

"Put your hand here, miss," the policeman said noncommittally. The Italian woman was still screaming, and she was told to be quiet. The Negro woman was moaning and praying to the Lord. Most of the men were silent. After the policemen who had brought them in and the sergeant at the desk had discussed what had happened, they were told they were going to be put in the lock-up overnight. "They can appear in court in the morning," the sergeant said.

"I didn't do anything," Kate pleaded. "My husband was hurt. I've got to know what happened to him."

"Tell it to the judge in the morning," the sergeant said.

A young man with a nice face, who Kate was sure must have been from O'Donnell's group, spoke to her. "He thinks he's doing us a favor by not sending us to night court. In the morning we can get a lawyer. Besides, you wouldn't like it at night court—it's full of junkies and drunks. Take it easy, kid. You'll be out in the morning."

Kate couldn't believe that she actually was going to be jailed overnight. What would happen to the Juarez family? She remembered with relief that she had given Mr. Juarez a key to the apartment, so he could get in when he arrived there with the truck.

Kate and the two women were put into a cell together. When the door was closed on them and locked, Kate broke down and cried. The fingerprinting had been bad enough, but now she felt as if her very identity as a person was being assaulted. How could such a thing happen to her? "I don't believe it, I just don't believe it," she sobbed.

The two older women tried to comfort her. The Italian woman put her coat on the wooden bench and made Kate lie down. "Go to sleep," she said. "Try to go to sleep."

Sleep seemed impossible, but after a while Kate did drift off. When she woke up she gave a start, not knowing where she was. Recognition of the bare, dismal cell with the light burning in the hall and a guard outside made her want to start crying all over again. But she didn't. She stretched herself to ease her cramped legs and sat down again. The other two women were dozing.

Kate knew she would never forget this night as long as she lived. She wanted very much for it to impart some deep meaning to her. But no revelation, no answers came. The only thing she could be thankful for was that while she was here the Juarez family was snug in her apartment. At least she had done that, and she was glad.

The hours dragged by. Kate dozed fitfully, and finally, although they had no window, she sensed it was daylight by some lightness in the hall. They were given lukewarm coffee and bread, and then each of them was allowed to make one telephone call. Kate tried to get Jake Bernstein, but she couldn't reach him, and she didn't know anyone else to call. The thought of going into court without a lawyer terrified her.

All the prisoners were taken over to the courthouse by the policemen who had arrested them. Now the groups separated. The two women and Kate, the nice-looking boy, and a couple of others drew together, while the rough-looking hecklers formed their own group, staring sullenly at the others.

Kate was frightened. She had never been in a court

before, and she didn't know what would happen to her. And she was worried sick about Mike. "Will they put us back in jail?" she asked the young man sitting on the bench next to her.

"I don't think so. I think one of the lawyers will be over to bail us out."

"Oh, I hope so," Kate prayed.

They were joined by some young men about Mike's age and a few girls like herself, who looked like college students. They seemed lighthearted and gay, and not particularly alarmed at being in court. "I've been in jail for demonstrating before," one young man said. "When I was at Harvard they took me off to jail."

"What were you demonstrating for?" Kate asked.

The boy looked at her in surprise. "For peace. That's why I'm supporting O'Donnell. He's for the same things I am. Isn't that why you're here?"

"I'm here because they hit my husband, and I got mad at the cop. I didn't really do anything. They just took me in with everyone else."

"That's too bad." But the boy gave her an odd look. "Which side was your husband fighting on?" he asked suspiciously.

"He's for Mr. O'Donnell. He's been working for him

night and day. He was bleeding when they took him away. I'm worried to death about him."

"He'll be all right." The boy was more sympathetic. "It's a tough neighborhood down here. They need a good man like O'Donnell to clean things up and get rid of some of the stinking tenements."

Kate was silent. She couldn't believe she was sitting in court with a bunch of strangers because she had hit a policeman, and that Mike, her husband, had been fighting on the street and carried off covered with blood. Hebron seemed like part of another world a million miles away. How can both kinds of life exist in one country? Kate wondered. What would her mother think if she knew? And the thousands of women like her mother, living in the tight, private, hemmed-in world of their home and their family, their marketing and their television shows, not knowing what was going on in the world and not caring. . . .

But then Kate thought of Mrs. Calgano, and Mrs. Juarez, and Mike's mother, and Tante Sara, and she was glad that she knew them—and maybe was one of them.

At last the judge came in. He was a middle-aged man who looked as if he wished he were home in his own house, instead of here dealing with people who had been senseless enough to get into trouble the night before. Watching him made Kate even more nervous. Then, with a tremendous sigh of relief, she saw Jake Bernstein enter the room. She had never been so happy to see anyone before in her life.

After that things moved swiftly. Several of the young men were let out on bail, arranged for by Jake, and Kate and the others were dismissed by the judge after he delivered a severe lecture to them.

"Where's Mike? How is he?" Kate had hold of Jake's arm.

"He's all right. They took him over to Bellevue. I was there. He's in the police ward. He's under arrest too, you know."

"What will happen to him? Can I go see him now?"

Jake answered her second question first. "Why don't you go home and rest a bit? They're not going to keep him in custody, so you can pick him up at the hospital around noon. I'll appear in court with him this afternoon. I think he'll get away with a light fine."

"You're sure he's all right?"

"Sure. Just a few cuts on his head."

Outside of the courthouse Kate remembered the Juarez family. She didn't really have a home to go to. But she had to change her clothes and get cleaned up, and she did want to see how they were. She said good-bye to Jake hurriedly and went home.

When she entered the door Kate felt an odd sensation at finding a whole family ensconced in the apartment that was hers and Mike's. She realized immediately she had done something Mike wouldn't like. Carefree as he was about many things, Mike was astonishingly fussy about his few possessions. The bookshelves had eventually gone up, and Kate had been surprised at the hours Mike had spent getting each book in exactly the right place. His desk was always in order, and it was Mike who occasionally on a Sunday would polish a lovely pewter pitcher they had been given for a wedding present.

Now the Juarezes and their belongings were scattered about. Their beds and bureaus had been left in the basement, but there were boxes of dishes and pots, piles of clothing, and blankets on the floor. The children had all been put into the bedroom, Jimmy had Mike's study, and Mr. and Mrs. Juarez had slept on the living-room floor on blankets. There wasn't a corner of the apartment that wasn't littered with either people or things.

"Is everything all right?" Kate asked. Mrs. Juarez was making coffee in the kitchen, and that room, too, was already covered with her jars of food and strange bags of fruits and seasonings, rags, and kitchen utensils.

"It is fine, it is fine." The Juarezes had been very worried about Kate until Jimmy had found out what had happened. The calm with which Mrs. Juarez accepted the fact that Kate had been arrested and spent the night in jail was to Kate the final bizarre touch to the night's proceedings. Cheerful Mrs. Juarez, with her cooking, her housekeeping, and her protective attitude toward little Carmen, took for granted that policemen arrested innocent people and that they spent the night in jail. Kate was too tired to be shocked by anything, but this last realization made her very sad.

12

KATE WAS AT BELLE-
vue Hospital by eleven-thirty. Having to sit and wait for
Mike to be discharged was nerve-racking. Everyone was
very polite, but the hospital procedure had to be followed
exactly. Finally Mike emerged into the waiting room.
"Darling, are you all right?" Kate lightly touched the ad-
hesive plaster across his temple.

"Sure. I'm fine. Let's get out of here. I hate hospitals.
And I'm starved. Let's go home and have an enormous
breakfast, or lunch. I have to meet Jake to appear in court
this afternoon, you know. And what do you say we
splurge on a taxi?" Mike was his usual exuberant self.

Kate's face clouded over. They were out on the street,
walking down First Avenue. It was a gray fall day, and

Kate pulled her raincoat around her against the wind. "I have something to tell you. We can't go home. Except to get our clothes." Hastily blurting the words out, Kate told him about the Juarez family. "They're there now," she ended up lamely.

Mike was speechless for a few seconds. "You are out of your mind," he finally gasped. "What a thing to do! You'll never get them out. How could you do such a thing without asking me first?"

"I didn't think you'd mind. It's only until they find a place. After all," she said, her anger rising in self-defense, "you're the one who's so concerned about people, who wants to make a better world. Well, now we're helping someone very specifically."

"But this is no way to do it." Mike looked at her in exasperation. "Giving one family a place to live for a few weeks doesn't solve anything. And what are we supposed to do? Stay at the Plaza, or live in Central Park?"

"I thought we could stay at Tante Sara's. She has a big house."

"And both of us travel from Brooklyn every day. Oh, Kate, you don't understand anything."

"That's what you say. I understand plenty." Hurriedly she told him of her experience the night before and of being in court that morning. "I spent the night in jail because of all the things you believe in. You care about the whole world, about everything except people! It's ironic beyond belief that you're the big hero, but I'm the one who went to jail."

"I'm sorry," Mike said, looking hurt. "But you didn't go to jail for me. Maybe you're beginning to find out that the world isn't as pretty as you thought it was."

"Don't start lecturing me." Kate was still upset from her night and morning's experience. She had been aching to find comfort in Mike's arms, and here they were fighting on the street like a couple of fishwives. "You're not willing to make any personal sacrifice. You never let me know when you bring people home to dinner, and now you can't take it that I lent our apartment to my friends. Maybe it will inconvenience you a little—"

"Inconvenience me a little! That's quite an understatement. Moving me out of my home, that's all. Besides, I object to the whole principle of the thing. You're acting like a sentimental martyr, evicting us for someone else. It makes no sense whatsoever."

"I am sick of your principles! This is the end, Mike. I can't take any more. I acted on my judgment and you don't agree. Well, that's too bad. I'm leaving. I'll take care of myself, and you can stay anyplace you want. I'm sorry I made a mistake in thinking I could count on you in a crisis."

Kate started walking rapidly and then running down the street away from Mike. "Kate! Kate!" she could hear him call after her. An empty taxi turned the corner, and Kate hailed it and got in. She caught a glimpse of Mike's dumbfounded face, watching her with stunned eyes.

Back in Mia's apartment, Kate gave vent to her tears. "It's no use," she sobbed. "We don't agree about anything. I thought he'd understand about the Juarezes, that he'd back me up."

"I think he was taken by surprise," Mia said gently. "Men don't like that kind of surprise. Besides, they like to think that they've been consulted and that they've made the decision."

"But that's ridiculous. We're living in the twentieth century. I'm not going to pretend that Mike knows everything and I don't."

"No, of course not. But I don't think things are all that different now between men and women from what they ever were, except that the male ego is frailer today. A man's ego used to be satisfied because he brought home the food, but you're doing it now, Kate, and Mike is going to be sensitive about anything that cuts him down. You not only pay the rent, you took it on yourself to give your apartment away. He must feel very unimportant."

"I hadn't thought of that," Kate said tearfully.

"There are a lot of things you haven't thought of," said Mia kindly. "I know things have been tough for you, physically tough, working and all. But they've been tough for Mike too."

"But he's had everything his way," Kate said stubbornly. "Mia, can I stay here for a while? There's a lot I have to think about."

"Of course you can, if that's what you want. We'd love to have you."

Against Mike's pleadings, Kate insisted that she wanted to be away from him for a few weeks. She stayed on with Mia and Gary while Mike lived at home with his family. The time was an unhappy period, for she missed Mike very much. But she also learned a lot. "I've never been on my own," she said to Mrs. Calgano. "I was either at home, or in a college dorm, or married to Mike. I guess I never really stopped to get to know myself very well."

One evening, in her restlessness, Kate was out walking alone. When she passed New York University a building was lighted up, and people were coming out of classes. But they were not the usual college crowd. Kate noticed middle-aged men and women and many elderly women with graying hair. They had tired faces, the faces of people who had worked all day. Kate realized that they were going to night school.

Impulsively she went inside, to see what she could find out about registering for courses. Though she acted on the spur of the moment, Kate knew the thought had been in the back of her mind for quite a while. If those older women could work and study, she could, too.

"I've decided to get my degree," she said the next day to Mrs. Calgano. "I need it for myself, and I certainly need it if I stay with Mike. I used to think that being married and having my own home and babies was all I would ever want out of life. But Mike has taught me one thing if nothing else. That those things aren't enough. Don't misunderstand me," Kate hastened to add. "I don't mean Mike is lacking. I mean that his own life is so full that I'd be lonely if I didn't have something of my own to fall back on. I think a lot of women are lonely, don't you?"

"I guess they are," Mrs. Calgano agreed. "I've never had the time to be."

Not anyone, not Mia or Gary or Mrs. Calgano, asked

Kate what her plans were. In a couple of weeks, when the Juarez family moved out—Mrs. Calgano finally found a place for them—Kate moved back into the apartment by herself.

On election night, when she came home from work, Kate knew she had made up her mind. Now, at last, she felt ready and able to cope with marriage. In her job at the Settlement House, in her decision to go on and get her college degree, and in the simple act of holding her ground on the matter of the Juarez family, she had found a strength within herself. She had something to give Mike now, something that they could both respect.

Kate had never been to Paul O'Donnell's headquarters before, and she approached the shabby building timidly. She had made up her mind, but what if Mike had changed his! During the time she had wanted to be alone she had only spoken to Mike a few times on the telephone. Maybe he had discovered that he liked being free. Maybe he had found another girl, like Peggy.

There was a tense excitement at the campaign headquarters. People were sitting around listening to the radio attentively, and someone was putting down the early returns on a blackboard. Mike, his face white and drawn, jumped up when Kate walked in.

"Hello," he said.

"Hello," Kate said. They looked at each other hesitantly, shyly.

"How's the election going?" Kate asked.

"We're doing okay. So far we're winning."

"I'm glad." With so many people around, Kate didn't know what to say. Mike's face was guarded. He looked thin and haggard, and his eyes told her that he had suffered as much as she. But she knew that he had done all his pleading. She was the one who had put him out, and she was the one who would have to say, "Come back."

"I'm back in our apartment," she said.

His voice was husky. "Is it *our* apartment?"

"If you want it to be." Her own voice was almost as low.

He didn't smile. For a minute Kate thought he might cry. She realized that it was going to take a long time before he lost that look of desperation. She wanted to take his head and bury it against her breast. But they stood there looking at each other, and then their hands clasped, and their fingers tightly entwined.

They sat with the others until after eleven o'clock, when the victory for Paul O'Donnell was conceded. The place went wild, but Mike and Kate sat together clinging to each other's hand, neither one wanting to let go. They were like a small island in the midst of all the cheering and excitement.

"Clear the tables—we're having a party!" someone called out. Mike and Kate got up from the desk where they had been sitting.

"Let's get out of here," Mike said.

"You don't want to stay for the party?"

Mike grinned, for the first time. "No, I don't want to stay for the party. Let's go home."

Hila Colman was born and grew up in New York City, where she went to the Calhoun School. After graduation, she attended Radcliffe College. Before she started writing for herself, she wrote publicity material and ran a book club. About fourteen years ago she sold her first story to the *Saturday Evening Post,* and since then her stories and articles have appeared in many periodicals. Some have been dramatized for television. In recent years she has turned to writing books for teen-age girls. One of them, *The Girl from Puerto Rico,* was given a special citation by the Child Study Association of America.

Mrs. Colman and her husband live in Bridgewater, Connecticut. They have two sons, one of whom is married.